DEADLY DRAMA

Molly glanced to her right and saw that the auditorium was empty. Looking back at the stage, she was surprised to see the house that had been suspended from the ceiling was resting in the middle of the set. Maybe they'd ended with that scene during their last rehearsal.

Molly wasn't thinking much of anything when she heard the hitch of a breath. Looking from the empty theater seating to the stage again, she heard another sharp intake of breath. She took quiet steps forward, brows scrunched at the sound of uneven breaths. Had she interrupted Magnolia crying? Molly hurried forward, moving around the open door of the hollow house.

A strange, strangled sound left Molly's mouth and her hands flew to her face, slapping hard against her skin.

Judd, the custodian she'd met a few nights back, was leaning over Magnolia's too-still body. Molly's heart tried to beat out of her chest as she realized the house was sitting at a slight angle. Worse, she saw why. Magnolia's feet were jutting out from bottom of the house, the rest of her body inside. It was a horrifying image of life imitating art, the house on top of the Wicked Witch of the West. Or, Britton Bay, in this case…

Books by Jody Holford

DEADLY NEWS

DEADLY VOWS

DEADLY RIDE

DEADLY DRAMA

Published by Kensington Publishing Corporation

Deadly Drama

A Britton Bay Mystery

Jody Holford

LYRICAL UNDERGROUND
Kensington Publishing Corp.
www.kensingtonbooks.com

LYRICAL UNDERGROUND BOOKS are published by

Kensington Publishing Corp.
119 West 40th Street
New York, NY 10018

All Kensington titles, imprints, and distributed lines are available at special quantity discounts for bulk purchases for sales promotion, premiums, fund-raising, educational, or institutional use.

Special book excerpts or customized printings can also be created to fit specific needs. For details, write or phone the office of the Kensington Sales Manager: Kensington Publishing Corp., 119 West 40th Street, New York, NY 10018. Attn. Sales Department. Phone: 1-800-221-2647.

Lyrical Underground and Lyrical Underground logo Reg. US Pat. & TM Off.

First Electronic Edition: August 2020
ISBN-13: 978-1-5161-1005-6 (ebook)
ISBN-10: 1-5161-1005-6 (ebook)

First Print Edition: August 2020
ISBN-13: 978-1-5161-1006-3
ISBN-10: 1-5161-1006-4

Printed in the United States of America

"All the world's a stage."
—William Shakespeare

Chapter One

Flowers were not her forte. For that matter, neither was wielding a camera. Today was a day of breaking out of comfort zones. Molly Owens adjusted the setting on the *Britton Bay Bulletin* camera and moved closer to the fat, yellow and blue blooms. There was something satisfying about the click when she captured the shot. She wouldn't look until later so she could hang onto the idea that maybe it was both artistic and functional.

Some of the tension from this morning had eased out of her shoulders just by taking a walk and getting out of the newspaper office, where she was editor in chief. But there was plenty left, hovering in the back of her mind and the base of her neck. Zooming out, Molly took a wide shot of the barrel and the flowers inside just as Calliope James opened the door to the Come N' Get It Café.

Her happy smile was just one of Britton Bay's treasures. "Hey, Miss Molly. What are you up to out here?"

Molly lowered the camera and turned to greet her friend. "Hey. Honing my photography skills using the Spring Flower Barrel challenge." Another Britton Bay tradition she was witnessing for the first time.

Calli pulled the key from the door, flipped her sign so it read open and then leaned on the doorjamb. "I heard you had some commotion over at the *Bulletin*. Doesn't sound like a pleasant morning, but sometimes these things are inevitable." She drew out the last word by enunciating each of the five syllables.

Molly couldn't hold back the smile even when the unpleasant memories from the morning filtered back in. "How on earth do you know that already? First, it only happened about a half hour ago and second, you just opened and haven't even seen a customer."

The owner, waitress, and town-knower-of-all-things pulled an elastic band from her wrist and began tugging her long red hair into a bun. "I have my ways, but this time it's because Elizabeth called in to place a lunch order for later today. She mentioned it, saying you all could use some comfort food."

The internet and social media combined were no match for small town gossip networks. If Calliope knew, the entire town would soon be updated on the status of their former social media coordinator and photographer. That status being: *fired*. Alan, who owned the paper, had agreed with Molly's opinions that Clay wasn't pulling his weight, brought the team as a whole down, and couldn't be trusted to follow through on assignments.

Molly had been the one to inform Clay, when he'd shown up forty minutes late for their morning staff meeting, that his services—or lack thereof—would no longer be needed. Though she'd expected him to be mad, she was shocked by his surprise.

"He had it coming. Get that look off your face," Calli said, stepping closer.

Molly shrugged. There were dozens of reasons to fire Clay. Molly had even written them down so she could *see* them on paper as backup. She wondered if finding Clay's father dead so many months ago would always weigh on her like an anchor of guilt. It wasn't her fault Vernon had died. Wasn't her fault she'd been the one to find him. As Calli would say: "These things happened." But Molly felt bad anyway.

"I expected mad. I didn't expect him to be shocked. I mean, we've been telling him for months that he needed to do more. Or just do his actual job. But he couldn't believe I was 'doing this to him.'" The camera moved against Molly's stomach when she let go of it to make air quotes.

"Honey, there are all types of people. But mostly, there's just two. Those who take responsibility for their actions and those who blame others."

Calli put an arm around Molly's shoulders and she leaned into her friend's warm half embrace. Calli was only a few years older than her, but she was exactly what Molly's mom would call an "old soul." She had a mother-hen-slash-best-friend vibe that drew everyone in. Just one of the many reasons the Come N' Get It was the most popular food spot in town.

"I know. That's a good way to look at it. What are these flowers called?" Molly pulled out her phone so she could take a couple of notes.

Calliope wandered over to the barrel and plucked a rather droopy looking petal off.

"These here are called cinquefoils. They're from the rose family."

Molly looked again, smiling at the heart-shaped blossoms on each flower. She'd planted them in the shape of a heart that took up most of the barrel.

"I'm pretty sure Katherine has something like this growing at the bed and breakfast," Molly said, referring to her landlord and boyfriend's mom. She'd need to pay more attention to her surroundings, something she was usually very good at.

Calli nodded. "She does. That woman has an emerald green thumb. How's things going with Sam?"

Molly couldn't hide her smile at the mention of her now-live-in-boyfriend who happened to be Katherine's son. "Wonderful. Speaking of, are you still good with the plan for her birthday?"

Sam's mom was turning sixty, and since she was one of Molly's favorite people and a beloved citizen of Britton Bay, they were planning a surprise party.

"Absolutely. I can't wait. You and Sam get her out of the bed and breakfast and we'll all take care of the rest," Calli said, yanking a couple of weeds from the barrel.

Molly leaned in to see if the flowers had a scent. "These really are gorgeous. I love the heart shape," Molly said. No one needed to be an expert to have an opinion on what was pretty.

"That's what I love, too. I enter to be part of the community. I never win because I keep my design simple," Calli said.

Calli's husband, Dean, came to the door of the restaurant. "You gonna talk all day or come in and get ready for the breakfast rush? Hey, Molly. How you doing?"

Molly smiled up at the tall, dark haired man. He was sporting a few days' growth. He wore a shirt that said: *No, really, Come N' Get It.*

"I'm good, Dean. I was just asking Calli about the flowers and taking some pictures."

Calli swatted his stomach even as she pressed up against his side. "Ignore him. He's only had one cup of coffee and he was up late last night helping to finish the construction of the set for the play."

Britton Bay might have been a quiet town but it surprised Molly how *busy* it was. They liked their festivals and events and activities. Their motto ought to have been *The more the merrier.*

"That's coming up soon, isn't it? I haven't been over to the center to check out the progress but I might later today," Molly said, thinking of photo opportunities. Jill was supposed to do a feature with the director, but the woman had put her off several times already.

"Good luck. Keep your head down when you go or you're likely to get it snapped off," Dean said. An atypical scowl creased his normally passive face.

Molly frowned, her brows arching up. "Not going so great? I've yet to meet the infamous Magnolia Sweet." She'd heard plenty about her though. From several sources.

"Let's just say she runs a tight, unfriendly ship," Calli said, checking her Fitbit.

"She doesn't smooth some feathers, she's likely to have a mutiny on her hands," Dean said, shaking his head. "She's an awful woman."

Molly was surprised by the venom in Dean's voice. He was as easygoing as Calliope was friendly. This woman must have really gotten under his skin. "I told Sarah I'd help with painting the set during rehearsals tonight. Maybe I should just stay backstage."

Two people wandered up the street—an older man and woman holding hands and laughing with each other.

"Look at this service, honey," the man said, his moustache twitching. "They hold the door right open for you."

"I told you this place was friendly," the woman answered.

Dean's features relaxed and he stepped inside. Molly moved back as Calli laughed, waving them in. "If you're looking for friendly people and delicious food, you are definitely in the right place. See you later, Molly. Duty calls."

Dean and Calli waved to her and Molly snapped another shot of the flowers for good luck. There had to be a couple of good ones. She continued down the sidewalk, waving to shop owners through windows as she snapped pictures of vibrant and varied barrels. The Spring Flower Barrel challenge encouraged all local proprietors to welcome spring with unique and colorful creations. So far this morning, Molly had seen flowers arranged in the shapes of hearts, a map of Britton Bay, houses, people, flowers, and the pier. The creativity blew her away.

Traveling around the world for her father's job in the Army had allowed Molly to see dozens of places around the globe. Between that and her own desire to pick up and move when the urge struck, she'd been something of a nomad. Until Britton Bay. This town, the people—one very good looking and sweet mechanic, in particular—and the community itself, had hooked her hard. For the first time in forever, she felt like she'd found a home.

Heading back to the *Britton Bay Bulletin*, she felt much calmer than she had when she'd left.

"There you are," Elizabeth, one of their feature writers, said. She was a lovely woman. Despite having no children of her own, she was the best friend of the owner's wife and quite motherly in everything she did. Molly adored her.

"Did you miss me?" Molly pulled the camera off of her neck and rolled her shoulders.

"Just worried you'd let Clay get under your skin," Elizabeth said, patting Molly's arm.

"I'm fine," Molly assured her, walking over to the layout table. It was mostly true. By the end of the day, she'd have shaken Clay's mood off completely. In the long run, they'd all have a more peaceful work environment without the troubled young man.

The Bulletin was another piece of Molly feeling tied to Britton Bay. She'd found the job posting online at a time in her life when she'd been looking for some direction. There'd been more than a few hiccups in the beginning, with Vernon's death and Molly's guilt-complex pushing her to solve the mystery of his murder. At first, she hadn't been entirely sure she was going to stay. Finding a dead body had a way of making a girl question whether or not she was in the right place. But the town had pulled together more than once in the face of tragedy and Molly felt connected all the way through to her bones. She'd never had what some would call roots, and this hundred-year-old perfectly square building had played a large role in giving her some.

"How you doing, Molly?" Jill asked, coming out of the back where there was a small kitchen, bathroom, and storage area. She held a large mug in both hands. It was the same pretty blue as the blonde woman's eyes, and matched her cheery nature.

"I'm fine. Honestly. I think I got some decent shots of the barrels," Molly answered, eager to shift the conversation to work.

In addition to Elizabeth, Jill, and Molly, the newspaper staff included Alan, the owner, and his niece Hannah, a high school senior who worked part time for them. Clay hadn't pulled his weight, but he had still done *some* things, which meant they were now strapped for bodies.

"Good. I'll download the pictures and take a look," Jill said.

Alan came out of his office, which was nestled in the corner of the main area that looked out onto Main Street. His salt and pepper hair looked like he'd run his hands through it several times already this morning. He'd lost the suit jacket and his tie, and had rolled his sleeves up to his elbows. His family had owned the newspaper since its inception and when Molly arrived, she'd been the man's last-ditch effort at salvaging his legacy. Fortunately for all of them, the paper was doing better than ever. But it wouldn't stay that way if they all ran themselves ragged.

"I've put in calls to a few people who've applied here in the past but I think I need to draft up something formal and get it online. We just can't keep up the pace we've been setting," he said, settling onto one of the stools around the layout table.

The main work area was a combination of desks, gray partitions, and a large layout table. They often gathered around it or in front of the whiteboard Molly had installed. Though the building was old, the huge storefront window brought in light and the smiles of passersby.

"I can reach out to my journalism professors and see if they can recommend anyone," Jill said, taking a seat beside Alan.

"That'd be great," Alan said.

Elizabeth joined them at the table, opening her day planner. Like Molly, Jill, and Hannah, she helped with the paper's online presence, but she preferred pen and paper to the calendar on her phone.

"I'll get a job posting up this evening," Molly said, uncapping a whiteboard marker.

She wrote down the stories they were currently working on, putting "Spring Play" at the top and following that with Barrel Challenge and Shop of the Month—a new feature they'd added to boost local businesses.

She glanced over her shoulder, looking at the others.

"Hannah is working on interviewing several graduates. If we start spotlighting them next week, we should be able to include the top ten in the graduating class," Alan said.

Molly wrote it on the board along with Elizabeth's reminder of the features she was doing on the addition being added to the high school, the acting mayor's plans for the community, and the upcoming election in which, if he ran, he was expected to win.

"That's a lot," Jill said. She sighed and set her tea down.

Molly capped her marker. "We'll be fine. I'm positive we can get someone in here by the end of the month. I can reach out and see if I know anyone who's willing to work remotely, do some of the editing so I can take on more of the stories while we're short staffed. Speaking of which, I'm helping Sarah and some of the others with the set tonight, so I can check in with the director about an interview."

One side of Jill's mouth tilted upward. "Good luck with that. Magnolia Sweet is not an easy woman to pin down and even when you do, she'd rather talk about her glory days as a Hollywood starlet than answer a question directly."

Molly sat at the table with them. "How long has she lived in Britton Bay?"

Elizabeth glanced up. "She's fairly new. About a year and a bit? She bought several acres up near Alan's home, but after a fall last year, she had to move into the seniors' facility at the edge of town. She has two children, but other than checking in on her home they don't bother much with her. Imagine being so cantankerous that even your own children don't want to be around you."

"She can't be that bad," Molly said. She'd glimpsed the woman a couple of times at the farmers' market. Both times, she'd worn ridiculously large sunglasses, wide-brimmed hats, and clothes that looked better suited to the red carpet than the beach. Molly figured she was just eccentric.

"Did you know she went to school at Britton Bay High?" Alan set his phone down and joined the conversation.

"What are you talking about?" Elizabeth's mouth dropped open.

He nodded, grinning. "Yup. Only for a short period of time, and then I guess she got a chance to audition for a soap opera and never looked back."

Jill picked up her tea. "Does her family live here?"

Alan shook his head. "Not that I know of. I think her parents moved here part way through the school year. She's a good fifteen years older than me, but I remember my uncle talking about how even back then she thought she was too good for this small town and anyone in it."

Molly leaned her forearms on the table. "Funny that she ended up returning then."

Life had a way of coming full circle. Molly wondered if some of the rumors she'd heard about Magnolia being a tyrant on set were exaggerated. She'd see tonight. If nothing else, the full circle angle would make for a great feature.

Chapter Two

By the time she walked home that evening, Molly had been in touch with a couple of people through friends of friends and had some leads on possible writers for *The Bulletin*.

As she turned onto the street where she lived, she caught sight of the sweet two-story Victorian home that housed the area's most popular bed and breakfast. She lived in the cottage out back. The owner, Katherine Alderich, really did have a green thumb. She took great pride in presentation. The grounds were immaculately kept, and though she wasn't participating in the Spring Flower Barrel challenge, there was an enviable number of flowers and blooms brightening up the yard.

Katherine stood on the front porch, chatting with two guests that were staying a couple more days. There weren't many bookings this time of year. Molly usually tried to sneak past when Katherine was playing hostess, but more often than not the woman brought her into the conversation. That was how she knew the husband and wife, laughing and sipping what was most likely tea, were here from New Jersey on business. Molly waved to all three of them and took the path down to her home. *Their* home. Her smile widened and the sound of a saw cut through the air.

Instead of going through the front door, she went around the side of the cottage that mirrored the main house and found Sam Alderich. He was not only an adored member of the community and Katherine's son but a magician of sorts. Somehow, he'd made Molly believe in words like "forever" and "always." They'd moved in together not long ago and though she'd had a few sleepless nights wondering if they were rushing, she couldn't deny that with Sam was her favorite place to be.

When the saw stopped, Sam straightened from the hunched position he'd been in and examined the cut.

"It's looking good," Molly called out so she wouldn't surprise him as she came through the back gate.

He turned and the smile he gave her made her heart catch. How? How did he do that every time? Sam set down the wood and walked over to her, leaned down and pressed his lips to hers in a sweet kiss.

"It looks fantastic now," he said with a grin.

She poked him in the admirably hard stomach and laughed. "Charmer."

"Doesn't mean it isn't true. How are you?"

"I'm good. Glad to be home," she said, not wanting to get into the day just yet. She stepped forward and wrapped her arms around his waist.

He hugged her tight, pressing a kiss to the top of her head. "I'm a little dusty. You're going to get dirty."

"Totally worth it." She snuggled into his chest.

Her back screen door shut and footsteps clomped their way. "Break time is over. Knock off the PDA," Chris, Sam's best friend and the acting sheriff of Britton Bay, said.

He handed Sam a can of cola and popped the tab on his own.

Molly stepped back and gave him a mock glare. "I'll remember that in a half hour when we go help Sarah on set."

Chris grinned and took a long drink. When he lowered the can, he reached out and tugged a strand of Molly's hair. She'd never had siblings but she imagined the affection and irritation she felt toward Chris was a good sample of what it would have been like.

"I'm the law around here. I have different rules," Chris said.

Sam snorted out a laugh and took a drink of his own soda. "Nice try, man." He hooked a finger in one of Molly's belt loops and tugged her closer. "You're still okay to go work on the set even after what happened today?"

Molly shook her head. "Why does this town even bother with internet? How on earth did you find out about Clay? I presume that's what you're talking about?"

Chris chuckled, set his pop down. "Will you always underestimate the local grapevine?" He began cleaning up the tools and wood. Sam and Chris were building a covered deck off of the back of the cottage.

"I don't. I know how fast it is, but really, how?" She stood with both hands on her hips while the two men cleaned up.

Sam winked at her. "Chris stopped in at Bella's to get some donuts to take to Sarah. Dean was grabbing a coffee, mentioned it to him."

Molly rolled her eyes and headed for the back door. "I'm not sure *The Bulletin* is even necessary. We'll be lucky if we can keep your mom's party a secret." She shook her head again. "I'm going to walk Tigger and then we'll head over?"

"Sounds good," Sam called after her. She heard the two men chatting and laughing through the screen door as it swung shut behind her.

Tigger, her adorable mixed-breed black and white dog, bounded out of his bed in the corner of the living area and barrelled toward Molly. It was quite comical, really, the way his legs moved faster than the rest of his body. He flopped down once in his efforts to torpedo her with affection. Going down on her knees, she rubbed his back and then his belly when he rolled over.

"Oh my goodness. It's like we've been apart for years. How are you, buddy? You good? Oh, I missed you, too. How about tomorrow you come to work with me?"

Work was where they'd found each other. The little guy had startled her behind *The Bulletin* when she'd parked and heard a strange noise by the dumpster. They'd adopted each other and Molly had been secretly thrilled when no one claimed the stray pup.

"Come on. Let's go for a walk," Molly said, getting up and going to the front door, the pup at her heels. Tigger's love of walks worked in Molly's favor since she was addicted to Calli and Dean's sea salt fries and the lemon loaf her friend Bella served at Morning Muffins.

"Just a quick one, bud," Molly said as they left through the front door. Despite the rumors she'd heard about the tension on set, she was eager to see the progress and meet the infamous Magnolia Sweet.

* * * *

Unless she stuck to the forested trails and away from the beach, no walk—with or without Tigger—was ever quick. Right after Molly had arrived in the small coastal town right outside of Portland, she'd found walking paths that allowed for privacy and went all through the hills along the beach. But the truth was, she preferred walking on the beach to walking beside it. Which inevitably meant stopping to chat with tourists and locals.

Tigger did not mind at all. Like her, he was a people person...or people dog. The trail from Katherine's house took her to a set of stairs that led down to a quieter area of the beach. She'd start there and head up to Main Street. Tigger loved the attention. He yanked on the leash, stopping Molly in her tracks and growled at a piece of driftwood partially covered by the sand.

Molly bent to retrieve it. "Really? You trying to show the stick who's boss?" She waved it in front of him, laughing at the way his tail wagging made his whole butt move. "Not so scary now, huh?" She glanced around quick and saw that there was no one close by. "One throw. That's it." She tossed the stick and let go of the leash at the same time, laughing when he momentarily got distracted by the leash following him. The tide was in but Molly didn't have much distance to her throw so it didn't matter. She remembered that Sam had been telling her about a summer baseball tournament he was part of. He'd asked if she wanted to join.

"I'll need to work on my throw a bit," she said out loud as the dog trotted back, tripping only once over his leash.

"Good boy. Look at you, conquering that mean stick." Grabbing the leash, they carried on with their walk. The sun was starting to set over the ocean, the colors blurring across the sky as the wind picked up. She loved the sound of the waves and the smell of the water. Surprisingly, to her at least, she loved the feeling that Britton Bay was *home.*

Molly stopped along the beach twice, once to let a little girl pet Tigger, simultaneously begging her moms for a dog. Both women shared amused glances with Molly while also loving Tigger up. They didn't say yes to their daughter's request, but Molly grinned when she walked away and realized they hadn't said no either. The second time was to say hello to one of the locals who was heading back from the pier, a fishing rod over his shoulder.

Molly loved the cadence of it all. There had been more than a few unpleasant moments in the town in the last eight months, what with three murders nearly back to back. It was unsettling to think of it like that in her mind, but she'd lived in Los Angeles, of all places, and had never experienced a dead body. Yet, here, in this town, she'd been part of solving not one, not two, but *three* murders. This was a large part of the reason why she and Chris, who'd gone from deputy to detective to acting sheriff in a very short period of time, often butted heads.

She didn't mean to get herself entangled in mysteries, but she couldn't deny they had a way of popping up when she was around. Despite the deaths, she felt safe and happy. Maybe there was something wrong with her that she could put those events in a box and store them on a shelf labeled *Do Not Think About*, but there was so much *good* about the town, it seemed to push everything else away.

"Hey Molly," Bella, owner of Morning Muffins, called out as Molly took the concrete steps up to the cobblestone walkway that would lead her part of the way home.

Bella was locking the bakery door, and turned all the way around as Molly got closer. "Hey. How's it going?"

Bella squatted down. "Hey, buddy. Sorry, no treats on me today." She looked up at Molly. "I'm good. How are you? Clay didn't get under your skin, did he?"

Molly laughed. "No. I'm fine. I am thinking that we just start sharing the news via gossip however, since it's the fastest source of communication around here."

Bella grinned unashamedly as she stood. "Nah. We still like to have something to look at online or hold in our hands."

Main Street was mostly shutting up for the night. When it wasn't tourist season, the hours shortened and the city seemed to sleep more. Molly hadn't noticed Callan's car when she'd stopped to say hello to the pretty brown-haired baker who made the best lemon loaf in the world. But she noticed his scowl when his car door opened and he stood up, looking at Molly and his on-again, off-again girlfriend.

"Hi, Molly. Bella, are we going or what?"

Molly cringed. She hated how Callan treated Bella. He could be a really nice guy but he could also be a complete jerk. Bella, on the other hand, was sweet and kind. She was always ready with a smile and a delicious treat, even when someone—say an editor who stuck her nose where it didn't belong—accused that on-again, off-again boyfriend of murdering the town's meanest reporter.

She'd admitted her mistake and apologized to both Callan and Bella but she'd never shaken the feeling that Callan was capable of dark things. He had an edge to him despite being friends with several of the people she knew and trusted.

Bella gave Molly a tight-lipped smile. "Better go. See you around."

Tigger whined as they watched her walk toward the car and get in. As someone who'd given too much of her life to a man who didn't deserve her, Molly's heart ached for her friend. But she knew from experience that Bella wouldn't and couldn't be convinced to walk away until she was truly ready.

She picked up her pace as she walked home, thinking that she also knew from experience that once a person let go of the negativity pulling them down—whether it was a person or something else—the world opened up its doors. Sometimes those doors led a person exactly where they were meant to be.

Chapter Three

The Britton Bay Recreation Center was a hub of activity when Molly, Sam, and Chris arrived later that night. With a big auditorium that included a stage, the town often held large-scale functions at the site. There were two small gymnasiums and several classrooms that offered a range of courses from seniors' yoga to CrossFit. Molly had tried a few classes but she preferred walking on the beach to a crowded, sweaty group workout.

A group of teens were heading noisily toward one gymnasium, a basketball bouncing in time with their steps. A couple of older women were paying for water yoga, which started shortly. A man and a woman who looked close to Molly's age stood waiting behind the women, arguing heatedly but quietly, both holding squash racquets. Chris and Sam waved to the young man behind the counter, who looked a little frazzled as he chatted with the customers.

The center was huge, with arms stretching out in each direction from the main area. The indoor pool was at the far end of one of those arms, but still the scent of chlorine hovered in the air, probably from people leaving after their swim. The three of them went to the left—clearly Chris had already come by to see his girlfriend, Sarah. She was a newer resident—which, to Molly, was anyone who'd settled in Britton Bay after her. Along with being a talented artist, Sarah owned an art studio up the road. She and Molly had become fast friends, which worked out well since their respective boyfriends were close.

"Through here," Chris said, gesturing to a set of double doors that had black paper taped over the windows. A white sign had been plastered over the paper saying, *Closed Set*. Molly bit her lip to keep from grinning. Apparently, community theater was a serious thing.

"You're not scared to go in?" Sam asked, gesturing to the sign.

Chris scowled. "This woman was on a soap opera for five minutes thirty years ago, and she acts like she's next in line for the throne." He tugged on the sign, pulling it down. "How on earth can she close the set when she needs volunteers to be ready for opening night?"

When he pulled the door open for them, Molly let Sam go first. "Sacrificing me?" he whispered as he led the way into the darkened auditorium.

"You're being noble," she whispered back, tucking her fingers in the back pocket of his jeans while her eyes adjusted to the dark.

"That's awfully nice of me," Sam said, reaching back for her other hand and pulling her close.

"You know what they say about nice guys," Chris whispered behind them.

Up ahead of them, at the front of the auditorium, the stage was lit up with overhead lighting but it didn't cast a glow far enough for Molly, Sam, and Chris to really see where they were going.

The door swung shut behind them, like it had been on a five-second delay. Everyone on stage froze and looked in their direction. If what Molly had heard about stage lighting was true, none of the cast could see them. Someone in the front row stood, almost cinematically slow, and turned. It was impossible with the distance and the dark to make out the features, and maybe it was the rumors she'd heard, but the figure looked ominous with the light glowing in the background.

"Uh-oh," Sam whispered, stopping. "I think we've upset the Wizard."

"What part of closed set do you not understand?" The slightly nasally feminine voice rang out through the auditorium like a dignified roar.

"We're here to help out with the set, Ms. Sweet," Chris called back. Molly could feel the tension radiating from him, nearly vibrating through the darkness. She'd been on the wrong side of Chris's anger more than once and knew he wouldn't cower in the face of conflict. They should have let him go first.

"Stagehands enter through the alley. *Never* through the front," Ms. Sweet called back.

Molly gulped down the ball of nerves that lodged in her throat. She'd been brave in the face of disaster more than once, yet just this woman's tone froze the hair on her arms.

"Maybe so," Chris said, stepping around Molly and Sam. "But there's a truck blocking that entrance right now."

"What?"

The director's shriek made Molly jump, and Sam pulled her into his side, putting his arm around her shoulder.

She pointed toward the stage, yelling, "Five-minute break. Not six; *five,*" and stormed off to what Molly was pretty sure was stage right. It wasn't until she got a bit further that Molly noticed there was someone following behind her. With the light and the dark, whoever it was had literally been eaten up by the former star's presence.

The three of them continued down the aisle toward the front of the room where the cast still stood like a scared tableau. Now that they were closer, Molly recognized several of the townsfolk including Sarah, who was crossing the stage with two cans of paint in hand, looking like she was holding back laughter.

Molly grinned at the people she recognized and tried to lighten the moment. "We're definitely not in Britton Bay anymore," she said loud enough for others to hear.

The laughter that rumbled through the cast and stage crew seemed to set them in motion. People started rushing off the stage to claim what was now the four minutes and thirty seconds they had left of their break.

Sarah greeted them as they ascended the short stairway up to the stage. She set the cans down behind the set.

"Hey." She went up on tiptoes to accept Chris's kiss, then leaned into him and looked at Molly and Sam. "I feel like I should tell you to run for your lives, but you know what they say about misery."

Sam and Chris chuckled while Molly looked around.

"There's safety in numbers," Chris said, a smile in his tone.

Sarah gave an exaggerated laugh, making Molly giggle. "That's what you think, my pretty."

Molly took a moment to absorb her surroundings. She'd been to a couple of community plays when she'd lived in other towns, but none had rivaled the elaborate detail of the set she was standing on. Instead of a stage, she stood on the yellow brick road, surrounded by tall trees of various shapes and colors. The wooden backdrop resembled houses on one side—meant to be Kansas, while on the other, Oz was depicted with an elegant castle. When she looked up, she saw a hollow house hanging in the air. Sarah stood beside her and pointed. "That's the house that kills the witch."

Molly looked at her friend, momentarily admiring the pretty green clip holding back her dark side bangs. "This is incredible."

Sarah nodded. "She's a tyrant, but she's actually very talented. I worked on plays all through high school and a bit in college. She knows what she's doing even if she doesn't go about getting what she wants in the nicest way."

Cora Lester— a local who'd informed Molly shortly after she'd arrived that by dating Sam she had stolen the perfect husband for her daughter— came to stand next to them.

"Don't be hard on Magnolia," Cora said. "Especially not where she can hear you. From what I've read, most geniuses have gruff personalities, and can you blame them? I mean, no one really gets them, do they?"

Before she could say anything in response, a tall woman dressed as Auntie Em glared down the bridge of her nose, even going so far as to put her fingers on her thin-framed glasses. For a moment, Molly thought she was just staying in character.

"Do you think all that brown-nosing will actually get you anywhere?"

Cora turned an icy shoulder on the woman and gave Molly a wide-fake smile. Molly knew from experience that Cora had a sharp tongue and didn't mind using it to spread gossip or warnings. It was surprising that she chose not to respond to the other cast member. Instead, she asked, "How are you, Molly?"

"Fine, thanks," Molly said, glancing over at Sarah.

The other woman walked away from them and Cora's smile dropped immediately. "You should really clear the stage for the actors," Cora said dismissively, pulling a folded script from her back pocket.

Sarah turned to Molly and rolled her eyes. "Come on," Sarah said. "I still have to paint the other side." As they moved around the wooden staging—basically long pieces of plywood artfully connected by two-by-fours at the bottom, Sarah looped her arm through Molly's. "She's one of the monkeys."

Molly stifled her laugh. Chris and Sam were already painting at one end of the panels.

"Everyone back in their places. I'm telling you, if every theater was this incompetent, there'd be no shows," Magnolia's voice rang out from somewhere out front.

"Where's Dorothy? Dorothy?" Her voice came out shrill.

"She refuses to call them by their real names," Sarah whispered, handing Molly a paintbrush.

Molly's eyes widened as an older woman she didn't recognize—and not just because she was dressed like Dorothy—hurried around the set and out to the front of the stage.

"Right here, Ms. Sweet," the woman said.

"Don't think I can't replace you," Magnolia said. Her voice carried well through the auditorium. "Let me tell you the first thing I learned in Hollywood; anyone can be replaced."

"Not you," Cora called back.

"I'm making a few changes. Dorothy, go stand stage left for a moment. Where are the monkeys? Instead of six, I only want three. Monkeys four, five, and six, you'll be silent woodland creatures instead. Tiffany, make a note."

Molly, glad she wasn't Tiffany— whoever that was— continued painting hand-drawn bricks a shiny shade of gold. Sarah's sharp intake of air made her look up. "You okay?" She whispered it across the space.

Sarah winced and pointed out front.

"But I'm monkey six," Cora said loudly.

"And now you're a quiet little bunny in the background. Let's go again with the lights. Is there anyone in the damn tech booth?" Fingers snapped loudly. "Anyone?"

"We're here, Ms. Sweet," said a voice through the speaker system.

"Finally," Magnolia said. "From the top."

"Ms. Sweet. There were no bunnies in the play. I don't understand."

Molly couldn't help it. She set the paintbrush down and tiptoed to the edge of the set, peering around. Several people milled about in the wings, and it felt like they were holding their collective breaths.

Magnolia came up the stairs and stood right in front of Cora. "Are you challenging me?"

Cora shook her head. "Of course not. It's just, I was pleased with my role."

Magnolia jutted out her hip and placed her hand on it. "And I would be pleased if you stopped wasting my time. While I was outside, I realized that the spark I'm missing isn't just because you're a dreadful lot of actors. It's because there are too many of you. No play needs this many active characters. Now, if you want to be part of the production at all, I suggest you hop along backstage and see if wardrobe has some cute ears for you to wear. Otherwise, your services are no longer needed. Tiffany, get me a water."

In the bright overhead lights, Molly caught the sheen in Cora's eyes, and though she was no fan of Ms. Lester, she felt badly for the woman.

"Well then. I quit. You think you can treat people however you want, Magnolia Sweet, but mark my words, one day it's going to come back and bite you in your butt."

Cora tossed her script on the ground and stormed off the stage. Magnolia spread her arms wide, looking around at the actors. "Anyone else? If you don't like the way I do things, you're free to go."

A waifish looking woman with her hair in long dark braids hurried over with a bottle of water and handed it to Magnolia, who snatched it from her hand and went to her seat. The woman followed.

No one else moved or spoke. Sarah joined Molly and whispered in her ear. "That's the second cast member who's left today."

Molly followed Sarah back to where they'd been painting, shooting Sam a smile she wasn't sure he could see in the low light. The actors began to rehearse.

"Who else?" Molly whispered as she kneeled down and swiped the brush through the paint.

Sarah picked up a can and poured more into the tray. "Lenora Ray left earlier today. She was supposed to be the aunt but kept mispronouncing words and Magnolia wouldn't stop yelling at her. It made Deb happy though. Do you know her? She lives at the seniors' villa out on the edge of town, where Magnolia lives. She's got a crush on Beau Harrison who plays the uncle."

Molly couldn't stop her jaw from dropping. "My goodness. It's like she brought the soap opera with her."

"Are people talking backstage? Stagehands, are you trying to ruin my production? You're back there to work, not yap all night. Again, from the top."

There were further moments of tension, but if Molly pushed that aside, listening to the lines from behind the stage was actually kind of fun. Careful not to talk and disrupt rehearsal, Molly and Sam shot looks to each other across the space. She had to stifle a laugh more than once as Chris and Sam goofed around in between working. Sarah shook her head repeatedly, her smile glimmering in the dark as she worked on the set.

By the time they'd painted the castle in full, rehearsal had come to a close. A man came through with a garbage can and a broom, his dark gray beard twitching when he passed Chris, Sarah, Sam, and Molly.

"You four hide out until the dragon lady left?" His eyes twinkled with amusement.

"You know me better than that, Judd. We aren't scared of her," Chris said, reaching out to shake the man's hand.

"Speak for yourself, man." Sam also shook the man's hand.

"You're not carrying your weapon, you ought to be scared. Though I reckon these lovely women could take care of you two scoundrels," Judd said, tilting an imaginary hat their way.

The guys laughed and Sam put an arm around Molly. "Judd here was our custodian when Chris and I went to high school. Now he keeps half the buildings in Britton Bay clean after hours. Judd, this is Molly, my girlfriend, and this is Sarah, Chris's girlfriend."

"Nice to meet you ladies. Sam, good, honest work never hurt anyone. You'd know all about that," Judd said, speaking to Sam with affection.

Chris took Sarah's hand but his chin popped up. "What about me? I'm good and honest."

Judd's eyes sparkled again. "You're acting sheriff, boy. That's next thing to a politician, so whatever good and honest you got left, you better hide it before the job takes that out of you."

The four of them laughed and Judd shared a couple of Chris and Sam stories from their youth, making them laugh harder.

"You kids go on. See you soon." Judd waved as he pushed the broom down the aisle and the four of them left the way they'd come in, this time without a hassle.

Chapter Four

Molly looked at the mock-up of the program Sarah had designed for the play. The four friends decided to try something different, heading just outside of town to a small pub called Outskirts. It was small but friendly, with music pumping through a speaker system, a handful of waitresses, and two bartenders. There was a dance floor in the middle of the room, which seemed unique to Molly. The bar took up the entire back wall of the place. There were booths along the two sides, with a hallway leading to the restrooms and tables surrounding the well-worn dance area. Currently, several couples were swinging each other around, just as the music suggested.

"This is fun," Molly said, gesturing to the program.

"Thank you. I hardly did any of it, though. Naomi drew all of that by hand," Sarah said with pride. Naomi was a nineteen-year-old who'd been letting herself into Sarah's art studio to use the materials. When Sarah found out, instead of pressing charges she'd arranged for the girl to work off what she owed. It hadn't taken her long, but Naomi had stayed on with Sarah. Molly was happy to learn that the formerly homeless teen was staying in a basement suite owned by Chris's parents.

"She's amazing. I love the cartoony way she represented the cast. So cute," Molly said.

The guys were discussing basketball, arguing over who would make the final four in the college league.

"How's she doing otherwise?" Sam asked, joining the conversation.

"My parents love having her downstairs. She's shy. Keeps to herself and goes to work. Pays her rent on time and planted a bunch of flowers for my mom," Chris said, his brow furrowing.

"Then why are you frowning?" Molly leaned into Sam, picking up her Strawberry Spirit Sipper. She didn't drink very often, but when she did she preferred sweet to sour.

"That's his default expression," Sarah said, gazing at him affectionately.

He laughed and slipped his arm around her shoulders. "Funny. I'd just like to see her become part of the community. She keeps to herself so much, sort of like she's ready to flee at any moment."

"She hasn't yet. Give her time. Sometimes the ones prone to take off and search for something new get sucked in and find a reason to stay," Sam said, his eyes moving over to Molly.

She poked him in the side. "Subtle." She'd been more than a little gun-shy about her relationship and the rate at which she'd fallen head over heels for the town's favorite mechanic. Sam was right though. Sometimes, all a person needed was a reason to stay.

"So, what's your take on Magnolia?" Sarah asked the group as the music switched to a slower pace.

Before Molly could answer, their server approached the table. "How are you four doing?"

He had a bright, engaging smile, slightly mussed dark hair, and more than a little hint of shadow across his jaw. With his tanned skin and dark eyes, he looked more like a model than a server, but as she knew, this was often a gateway job for college kids.

"We're good. Actually, you guys want to share some nachos?" Chris asked, looking around the table. When the others nodded, he looked back at the server. "A plate of nachos, no olives or onions, please. And I'll take another cola."

The guy nodded, then glanced down at the program. "Oh, that's fantastic. Are you guys part of the play they're putting on?"

Sarah shook her head but offered, "We're just helping out backstage. None of us are actors. Are you?"

Molly caught Chris's frown at Sarah's question and almost laughed but Sam caught her attention by slipping his arm around her shoulder.

The waiter picked up the program and opened it, obvious admiration in his gaze. "No. Not at all. But I love the theater. I'm writing a play, actually, and I stopped by to see if maybe I could chat with the great Magnolia Sweet. You know, ask for some pointers? I'd read online that back in the day, she wrote a few episodes of the soap she worked on." He set the pretty program down and shook his head like he was shaking off a memory.

Molly's guess was that it wasn't a pleasant memory if Magnolia was involved.

"Uh-oh. How'd that go?" Sam asked, picking up the same vibe as Molly.

The server gave a humorless smile. "You work backstage? I'm betting you can guess. Oh well. That's what online courses are for, right? I'll be back with your drink." He hurried away from the table and the gears in Molly's brain turned, shifting into place.

She leaned in and kissed Sam's cheek, then scooted out from under his arm. "Back in a minute."

She followed their server to the back of the bar, impressed with how quickly he weaved in between the tables and around patrons, and still managed a smile and wave for customers. When he stopped at a table right before the bar, he caught sight of Molly and frowned.

"Did you need something besides nachos?"

Molly pulled in a breath and spoke over the music. "You said you're a writer? I was wondering if it was a hobby or a profession." She'd always believed in signs. One she'd stumbled across online at three in the morning, sitting in a dowdy motel room, unable to sleep, had brought her where she was today.

He grabbed a couple of empty glasses off the table and straightened, looking down at Molly with suspicion in his gaze. "A little of both, but mostly the former while I work toward making it the latter."

Molly grinned. "You work here full time?"

He glanced around toward the table she'd just left, then back at her. "No one works full time. They have to pay benefits that way. Listen, lady. I'm flattered but I don't date people I meet at work and your guy seems really cool."

With a heavy guitar riff opening up the next song and Molly's shock blocking her speech, it took her a minute. "What? No. Oh my gosh. I'm sorry. I'm not...hitting on you or asking you out. Oh my goodness." She wondered if he could see the deep shade of red she felt herself turning.

"Uh...okay," he responded with a slight wince. "My bad. Sorry."

Molly forced herself to laugh off the embarrassment rolling over her in waves. "Let me try this again." She stuck out her hand. "I'm Molly Owens, editor-in-chief for the *Britton Bay Bulletin*. We're looking for writers for our newspaper as we're currently very short-staffed."

His expression morphed into one that made him even more handsome. Not that she was interested. At all.

He took her hand and shook it. "Ahh. Okay." He laughed. "Gavin Bright. Nice to meet you, Miss Owens."

She shook her head and laughed. "Molly." She glanced back and saw her friends and boyfriend watching her with amusement. Yup. She loved to provide amusing anecdotes. They were going to love this one.

When she dropped her hand, she let out a relieved sigh. *Awkward moment mostly gone.* "If you do any freelance writing, I'd be happy to take a look at a sample. I'm not sure if you're looking for work."

"Any writer knows that the only thing better than writing is getting paid to do it. I don't have anything on me but could I email you? I'm definitely interested, though I've never done any investigative pieces or anything. I'm actually finishing up my creative writing degree." His voice lowered like he was somehow embarrassed by that fact.

"You can absolutely email me. That'd be great. Go through *The Bulletin's* website and I'll get it. Sorry about the misunderstanding."

"My fault. I'll go get your nachos ordered. Thanks, Molly. This is really cool."

He smiled and walked the rest of the way to the bar. Two people came up behind Molly and asked if she was saving the table.

She shook her head and hurried back to their table. When she slid onto the padded bench seat, the others stared at her expectantly.

"Do I need to beat him up?" Sam asked, reaching out to twirl a lock of her brown hair around his index finger.

Molly laughed and leaned into him, inhaling the familiar and sexy scent of his cologne. "Absolutely not. Especially if he's a good writer."

Sarah clapped her hands together. "Oh. Right. He said he writes plays. Good call. We couldn't figure out what you were doing."

Molly's face heated again and she buried it in Sam's shoulder as Chris commented, "I spend a fair amount of time wondering exactly that."

Sam pressed a kiss to the side of her head and then his lips brushed against her ear, sending a shiver through her body. "Just one of the many things I love about you." His words were quiet, meant just for her and they drowned out the lingering remains of embarrassment.

She tilted her head back and hoped that her mutual feelings shone in her gaze. They must have, because his grin widened and he pressed his mouth to hers in a sweet kiss.

They chatted about the play, other events coming up and a number of other topics with the ease of good friends. By the time their nachos arrived, Molly was feeling more than a little happy. She felt content.

"Here you go," Gavin said, setting the nachos in the middle of the table and a cola in front of Chris. He looked at Molly. "Thanks again for asking about the writing. I'll email you right after work." He frowned. "Not that you have to check the email then. Just that—"

Molly lifted her hand as Chris's phone buzzed on the table. "No worries. I look forward to reading your sample."

"Awesome," Gavin said. "You guys need anything else?"

"We're good. Thank you," Sam said.

While the others loaded their plates, Chris stared at his phone and then swore softly. Sarah put her hand on his arm. "You okay?"

He shook his head. Molly recognized his look. Something was wrong. "I need to go."

"Oh," Sarah said, her lips tilting down. She set her chip down and picked up her purse.

Chris shook his head. "No. You guys stay. Sam, one of the deputies will pick me up. Can you take Sarah home when you finish here?"

"Sure, man. Everything okay?"

Chris sighed heavily and leaned in, his forearms crossing on the table. "There's some trouble out at the Granger farm. It's the third time this month. Someone is coming into the barn and upsetting the animals but we haven't been able to catch anyone. I asked John to install cameras but the most he'll do is motion lights. He says he isn't paying to install cameras on his own land so the government can have an easier time watching him."

The three of them laughed but Molly wondered if Chris ever got tired of putting out proverbial fires. If he took over as permanent sheriff, his responsibilities would only increase. Looking across the table at Sarah and noting the slightly forced grin on her friend's face, she couldn't help but wonder how this sort of thing impacted a relationship.

Chapter Five

Molly pulled the door to Morning Muffins open, feeling only a tiny bit of guilt. She probably spent a good portion of her paycheck on eating takeout. But it was *so good.* By far, Morning Muffins and Come N' Get It were her favorite stops. The bakery was already busy with four customers in line and several others dotted around the small space, sitting at high, round, bar-style tables with their warm beverages and delicious snacks.

Bella was a culinary genius. Molly must have shared this truth a fair amount, because when her mom and dad had visited at Christmas time, they'd insisted on tasting the scones she'd described as life-changing and the lemon loaf that was too good to properly articulate.

Fishing her wallet out of her purse as she got in line, Molly waved to a couple of locals. The woman in front of her pulled her phone from her pocket. It must have buzzed because it hadn't rung, and she put it to her ear.

"Tiffany, speaking. Yes ma'am. I'm grabbing the muffins you asked for. No. No. I'm just waiting in line." The woman sucked in a sharp breath. "I can't do that. There are only a few people in front of me. Yes. Okay." She held the phone away from her and glared at it.

Molly caught sight of her profile. She had flawless, pale skin that seemed almost ivory next to her jet-black, flowing hair. She had sharp cheekbones and a brow so furrowed it was easy to spot even from the side.

"Goodbye to you, too. And I'm fine this morning. Thank you for asking, you crazy, raving—"

"Next," Georgie, one of Bella's staff called.

Molly's eyes widened as they each moved a step forward and the person who'd just paid left the line. The woman in front of Molly—Tiffany—

flushed, probably realizing too late that she'd spoken out loud. She glanced at Molly and her cheeks reddened further.

"Sorry."

Molly grinned. "Don't be. I've had my share of evil bosses." It was a hunch, but Molly was pretty good with those.

"How'd you know?" Tiffany shoved her phone back in her pocket.

"You called the person ma'am, looked to see if you could move things along faster, and waited until she hung up to share your thoughts."

Tiffany laughed, tipping her head back, turning her features from lovely to striking. When her eyes found Molly's again, they sparkled, looking like blue diamonds. "Are you a detective?"

Molly shook her head, grateful Chris wasn't around. "No. Editor at the newspaper and sometimes writer."

"Next," Georgie called. "Oh, hey, Molly!"

Molly waved at the young girl. *Young? She's less than ten years younger than you.* Molly would be thirty at the end of this year, and somehow just thinking that made her feel eons away from where Georgie was in her life.

"Hey, Georgie. How's school?" Georgie was attending a college about forty-five minutes away to get her business degree. She was one of Bella's best apprentices, but Bella had told the girl she needed more than baking skills to run a business.

"It's good. Hi. What can I get for you?" Georgie asked the next customer.

Tiffany wasn't a common name, and Molly had made the connection almost immediately after she'd announced herself into the phone. She hesitated for only a moment. There was only one customer left in front of the woman.

"So, you're working on the play with Magnolia, right?"

Tiffany turned, holding her large purse against her chest, her wallet clutched between her hands. Her eyes lost all of their shine.

"I am. I'm an assistant." She frowned. "More of a servant, really but everyone pays their dues, right?"

"You're not wrong. I worked my share of lousy jobs before I landed the one I have. I'm Molly, by the way."

"Tiffany. And that's what I keep telling myself. Every single day. You look a bit familiar." Her brows scrunched again like she was trying to place her.

"I was on set the other night, helping a friend paint."

Tiffany smirked. "Ahh, yes. The intruders."

"Next," Georgie called.

Molly laughed, her pulse scrambling a bit. Tiffany might be the closest thing to an interview *The Bulletin* could get.

"Hi there. How are you?" Georgie asked.

Tiffany's shoulders stiffened. "Oh. I'm fine, thank you for asking. Uh, I'll get two low-fat bran muffins, in separate bags please, a regular tea steeped for two minutes exactly and...oh my, is that a chocolate croissant? No. I'll get a low-fat blueberry muffin in its own bag please."

Georgie nodded cheerfully and set about gathering the order. Tiffany turned back to Molly and shrugged and rolled her eyes. "Easier to annoy others than not get her highness what she wants. She'd just make me come back for another if it's not perfect."

"Speaking of your boss, we'd love to do a feature on her for the paper but she's been hard to pin down. I know she's busy with the play so we didn't want to push too hard." *Plus, Hannah and Jill are scared of her.* Hannah had started doing more interviews and could handle the exchange easily if the person was accommodating, but Molly would never send the twelfth-grade student to interview Magnolia.

Tiffany's features hardened, suddenly resembling smooth granite. "You have to frame these things just right. If she feels like you want something from her or don't appreciate who she is, she'll blow you off. I could probably answer most of what you'd want to ask." She glanced over to where Georgie was steeping the tea. "No more than two minutes, please."

Georgie smiled and pulled the tea bag out. "Perfect."

She probably has to field questions all the time. Molly ignored the sudden chill of Tiffany's words. "I'd love to ask some questions if you have time, but do you think there's any chance she'd be willing to answer a few?"

Tiffany eyed Molly for what felt like a long minute. She paid for her order, tucked her wallet away, tugged the strap of her purse over her head so it rested on top of her jacket and picked up her items. She sighed, her mouth and gaze softening a touch when she looked at Molly.

"I can't promise anything but she's at the theater early every day. Says she needs to clear her mind and connect with the space without any of us there ruining it. Do you think you could be there at, say, four today? I'll mention it and say you've been dying to talk to her about her days as a star. That's what really makes her shine."

Molly nodded. "That would be fantastic. Thank you. I'll be there at four."

"Good luck." The right side of her mouth tipped up and Molly got the impression she might need that luck.

"Thanks. Nice to meet you," Molly said, too excited to realize the woman never said it back.

She approached the counter and grinned at Georgie. "Bella not working this morning?"

Georgie leaned forward. "She's in the kitchen working on Katherine's cake. Wait until you see it."

Molly's brows shot up. "Really? The party isn't for three days."

More customers walked in and the bell over the door jingled in competition with Georgie's cute laugh. "It goes in the freezer while she decorates. Don't worry, she's an expert."

Rubbing her stomach, Molly nodded. "That much I know. I'm going to have to switch to yoga pants only if she becomes any more of an expert."

They chatted another few seconds before Molly placed an order for enough food to share with her co-workers. Those walks she took Tigger on were more than just his exercise; they were Molly's free pass to enjoy all the good eats Britton Bay had to offer.

* * * *

Molly expected the rec center to be on the quiet side when she arrived just before four. The parking lot, however, suggested otherwise. As Molly got out of her beloved blue Jeep, she looked up at the moody gray sky, wondering if she'd get to take the top off early this year or if the winter chill was going to hang on tight.

Hitching her bag on her shoulder, she turned, locked the Jeep, and stopped in her tracks, brows coming together as she looked across the lot. Was that Tiffany getting into the passenger's side of a Honda CRV? The long black locks of hair hanging from a ponytail made Molly sure it was, but the person was quickly inside the vehicle with the door shut. Weird. This morning, when she'd said Magnolia didn't like anyone else in the theater, she assumed they all arrived later in the evening. Hopefully, she'd smoothed the way for Molly to get some questions answered.

Looking up at the bright sky, she wondered if Tiffany lived in town or just came to Britton Bay for the play. Molly walked toward the front door, then thought better of it and went around the back. As she padded along the narrow alleyway, where the truck had been blocking the door a few nights earlier, she crinkled her nose at the strong smell of garbage.

The door to the back of the auditorium wasn't locked, which Molly found helpful. She let herself in, making sure it was shut behind her.

The quiet, dark hallway was ominous and sent a shiver over Molly's skin. She rubbed her arms through her lightweight jacket and walked along the barely lit narrow corridor toward the stage. The other night, she'd run off stage to grab a couple of extra brushes Sarah had needed, so she knew the hall led to the stage and out to a side door for the auditorium. There were a bunch of extra rooms and closets off of the hallway but, as Tiffany had said, no one was around.

When she made it to the door that opened to the auditorium, Molly pressed the handle and frowned. It wouldn't budge. Looking down, she saw it had been locked from the bottom. *Maybe so people don't come backstage?* Although, she realized, they could use the stage stairs if they really wanted to.

She hoped Magnolia didn't have some sort of meditation ritual or something that she'd be interrupting. Did she just sit in the audience seats and stare at the stage? The door to it, also shut, showed light from the gaps. And it was unlocked.

Molly didn't mind doing interviews, even though she preferred editing and organizing at the paper. Nerves weren't usually an issue for her even when meeting new people. Other than Sam. That man had sent butterflies all the way through her at first sight. She smiled, thinking of him as she ascended the stairs at the side of the stage. She couldn't wait to see the changes to the set that had occurred over the last couple days. Sarah told her that every day, the scenery and the background came more and more alive, and that by opening night they'd feel like they really were in Oz.

This side of the stage would be closed off with one set of the large black curtains currently tucked away with a thick...cord that didn't match the red velvet ropes on the other side. She wondered, momentarily, if any sort of fund raising occurred to help the recreation center. They could probably use it. She'd have to ask Sam and Katherine.

Molly glanced to her right and saw that the auditorium was empty. Looking back at the stage, she was surprised to see the house that had been suspended from the ceiling resting in the middle of the set. Maybe they'd ended with that scene during their last rehearsal. Its door was propped open and it had been fully painted. The fact that it actually had a working door was one more nod to the effort people had put in to make this production a success. Molly wasn't thinking much of anything when she heard the hitch of a breath. Looking from the empty theater seating to the stage again, she heard another sharp intake of breath. Trepidation zipped through her blood and the tiny hairs on the back of her neck stood to attention. *Please don't let me be interrupting something important.* Molly wanted to start off on the right foot with the woman. She took quiet steps forward, brows scrunched at the sound of uneven breaths. Had she interrupted Magnolia crying? Molly hurried forward, moving around the open door of the hollow house.

A strange, strangled sound left Molly's mouth and her hands flew to her face, slapping hard against her skin.

Judd, the custodian she'd met a few nights back, was leaning over Magnolia's too-still body. Molly's heart tried to beat out of her chest as she realized the house was sitting at a slight angle. Worse, she saw why. Magnolia's feet were jutting out from the bottom of the house, the rest of her body inside. Molly saw her eyes were closed and her arms were bent, like she'd been holding them up by her head. Molly stepped back, shaking her head even as Judd started to rise, tears in his eyes, and she realized, with a tiny bit of physical distance, that if the door were shut, the only thing someone in the audience would see was a pair of boot-covered feet. It was a horrifying image of life imitating art, the house on top of the Wicked Witch of the East. Or, Britton Bay, in this case.

Molly had already pulled her phone from her pocket and started to dial 9-1-1 before her brain could catch up with her hand. Her foot nearly shot out from under her and when she glanced down, she saw she'd slipped in a puddle of brown liquid...coffee? She didn't see a cup. Looking back up, the air froze in her lungs. Judd had moved quickly and was coming closer at an alarming speed as Molly continued to back away. She screamed even as the operator picked up.

Chapter Six

Judd gripped Molly's wrist, his fingers digging into her skin with his hold. Her body jolted mid-fall and felt suspended for several seconds before he yanked her forward, away from the edge. The phone jostled against her ear.

"Ma'am? Can you tell me your name? Can you hear me?" The operator's voice was steady and strong. Sobering.

Judd released her wrist, his face twisted with sadness. Tears welled in his dark eyes.

"We need ambulance and police at the rec center. There's been a...a..." She stared at Judd and he waved her toward the body, shuffling closer.

"She was like this when I found her," he said, his words wobbling. He stopped near Magnolia's feet. "Don't know that an ambulance will do her much good now. I checked her pulse."

"Ma'am, are you in immediate danger? We've dispatched police," the operator said.

"No. I, uh, there's been an accident."

Judd nodded his head and pulled a white handkerchief from the back pocket of his jeans, using it to wipe his brow and then his eyes.

"Police are on their way. Are you alone?"

"No." She pulled in a deep breath. Her pulse settled to a simmer rather than a rapid boil. Judd stood near the body, pulling the handkerchief through his hands, one to the other. Molly took another deep breath. "No. My name is Molly Owens. I'm with Judd Brown and it looks as though Magnolia Sweet has died."

She didn't register what the operator said after that because she hung up, slipping her phone in her back pocket. Her hands shook and her steps didn't feel quite steady.

"Are you all right?" she asked him, keeping her distance but scanning the stage.

He scoffed. "Better than her, obviously. You think it just fell on her?" He looked up to the ceiling then leaned into the house again.

She didn't want to look but her feet took her closer. "There's no head wound." Her eyes scanned the ground. Nothing she could have tripped or slipped on. If she'd slipped on the same coffee Molly had, she wouldn't be lying where she was.

Judd continued running the cloth through his hands with increasing speed. "Maybe the fright of it killed her."

Unlikely. From what Molly had seen and heard, not much scared this woman. Other than the fact that she was lying with a house on top of her legs, Magnolia looked peaceful. She lay unmoving in a purple turtleneck and black slacks. There was something white under her head. A white cloth of some sort. But no blood, no marks. She took a step away, her eyes scanning the rest of the stage. It looked complete and oddly enchanting.

Taking a deep breath, she looked up at the rope, slowly moving around the house to see if maybe the rope was frayed. Had it just fallen? A scrap of blue stuck out from where two sides formed a corner. Molly leaned in to see what it was but jumped back with a shudder as she heard the sirens. Within seconds, police were coming through the front of the auditorium, Chris leading the pack.

She felt them approach from the side even before one of the officers barked out, "Freeze. Both of you stay exactly where you are."

"For the love of," Chris stopped and stared at her. "*Molly.* Dammit. Judd? You okay?"

She frowned and turned to face Chris. "Why would you just ask him if he's okay?"

Chris holstered his weapon and instructed the others to do the same, coming around the side of the stage and taking the stairs two at a time.

He gave Molly a look that could turn water to ice. "Maybe because he doesn't make a habit of finding people like this."

Irritation buried the rest of her shakiness and she squared her shoulders even as she crossed her arms over her chest.

He sighed, pinching the bridge of his nose as the other two officers who'd come in behind him went to the body and the officer who'd yelled at them went to Judd.

"I don't do it on purpose," Molly said, forcing the words through clenched teeth.

Chris shook his head and sighed deeply. "I know you don't."

He looked over at his guys. Molly recognized Officer Trevor Wills. He was another newbie to the area, though not to the job. He glanced at her, his lips pressed into a tight line, then met Chris's questioning gaze and shook his head.

"Call the coroner. Secure the scene." He put both hands on his hips, his brows practically touching.

Molly worried for one quick minute she'd be responsible for Chris having a stroke. Fortunately, he was young and pretty used to her. He pulled in a deep breath, hung his head and exhaled. When he looked back up, he appeared deceptively calmer.

He even gave her a one-sided smile. "Well, Ms. Owens. You definitely know the drill."

Molly curved her lips in a false smile, refusing to cower even though her body felt cold. She reminded herself that Chris actually *liked* her and he did have a point about finding bodies.

"I do. Would you like me to give you my statement or your deputy?"

"I'll take it. Start talking."

That was not something he said to her all that often.

* * * *

Molly was grateful that Chris let her phone Sam after her statement, even though he didn't want her to leave just yet. She sat in the front row, her heart and limbs equally heavy. The theater was lit up like a Christmas tree during the winter festival. It was nearly blinding and quite warm. Molly removed her jacket as Sam hurried over to her. She hadn't seen him come in since she'd stopped paying attention to the comings and goings; her mind was somewhat numb. His mother was right behind him.

She stood and practically fell into his arms. He scooped her up against him, burying his face in her neck. He pulled back, looked down at her, looked her over, and then met her gaze.

"You're okay?"

Before she could answer, Katherine swatted him away and took Molly's face between her hands, turning it one way and then the other as if inspecting it for damage.

"You're fine?"

Molly nodded and leaned in to hug Katherine. "I promised your mother I'd keep you out of trouble. Please don't make me a liar," Katherine whispered.

Molly pulled back and gave a watery laugh. Sniffling she leaned into Sam, whose arm came immediately around her shoulder.

"Trust me, I really don't mean to. This was truly a case of wrong place and time. For both Judd and me. And, unless she did this to herself on purpose, Magnolia, too."

Sam looked over to the stage, his jaw tightening. Magnolia's body had been taken away but Chris's men were still photographing every inch of the stage and interviewing the actors and stagehands who'd shown up for rehearsal.

"Chris thinks it was an accident?" Katherine asked, flanking Molly's other side.

Molly's nod was followed by a shrug. "I think so. She has no head wound though. Maybe she had a heart attack. It doesn't make sense," she muttered.

Sam's hand rubbed briskly up and down her arm before he turned her toward him, looking down at her again. "You're shaking. The adrenaline is wearing off."

Chris, who'd been over near the left side of the stage talking on the phone, walked over to them as he slipped his phone in his pocket.

"Hey," Sam said.

"Sam. Ms. Alderich."

Sam's mom patted his cheek and squeezed his forearm. "Christopher, you call me Katherine for heaven's sakes."

Molly bit the inside of her cheek because everything felt funnier when she was punch drunk. It wasn't late but she was exhausted. The kind of boneless fatigue that typically followed a fast and furious rush of endorphins.

"Yes, ma'am. How are you doing, Molly?" Chris asked, sounding as tired as she felt.

"I'm okay. Where's Judd? Is he all right? He was so shaken up when I got here." Molly lifted her hand to brush the hair out of her eyes. It was falling out of the ponytail she'd pulled it into hours earlier.

Chris scowled and reached forward, his hand grabbing her elbow.

Sam scowled back. "What are you doing?"

Molly blinked rapidly. What was he doing?

With a gentleness she didn't expect, Chris took her hand and stretched her arm out, rubbing his thumb over her wrist. She hadn't noticed the bruising until then.

Deep, dark, purplish bruises marred her skin. On top, it was a nearly solid band of discoloration, but when Chris carefully turned her arm over, the other side showed finger imprints.

"Who did this to you?" Chris snapped.

Molly thought it was weird that she'd felt just fine—other than sleepy—until that exact moment. Now, her wrist throbbed. "Oh. Uh, when I got here, I was so startled I backed away from the body, and I guess I was going to fall off the stage. Judd grabbed me so I wouldn't."

"You *guess*?" Chris asked as Sam put a hand on her shoulder.

"I didn't realize I was so close to the edge. He saved me from falling."

"And left one hell of a mark," Chris said, letting go of her hand.

Molly encircled her wrist with her other hand, feeling the gentle heartbeat under those fingers. She stared at the marks a moment, again wondering how Magnolia could look so peaceful, not a scratch on her, and not be okay.

She lifted her chin and looked at Chris. "The mark would have been worse if I'd tumbled off the stage."

Katherine rubbed Molly's arm. "Thank God you didn't, sweetheart. Chris, we need to take her home. She's about to fall over. Surely, you're finished with questioning." It was a prim and firm motherly tone.

"Yes, ma'am. Go home, Molly. Get some rest…and do me a favor?"

She sighed, long and deep. "Like you said, I know the drill. I won't print any details until you give me some."

"That's right. I'll let you know the cause of death when I do but until then, let's respect the family in their time of grief."

Molly bit her bottom lip to avoid snapping at him. She might be a lot of things—dogged, stubborn, and—now and again—a teensy bit reckless. But she was never thoughtless or careless about people's feelings. It came from having people be that way about her own so often throughout her life. From new school mates to boyfriends, people had opted not to tread carefully where Molly's heart was concerned.

"Have they been notified?" Sam asked.

Chris nodded. "Yes. But that's all I can say. Go home. I'll speak to you later."

"I'll count the minutes," Molly answered, picking up her coat and purse. She caught Sam's gaze and her heart tumbled in her chest. He was looking at her with so much affection she had to fight the urge to throw herself at him again.

"Cute," she heard Chris mutter as he walked away.

Katherine took Molly's purse from her and gently pulled Molly's long, dark ponytail from beneath the collar of the jacket Sam helped her slip on.

"Why do you and Chris constantly push each other's buttons?" she asked as they walked toward the exit of the auditorium.

"Everyone needs a hobby," Molly said around a yawn.

Three police vehicles were parked in the loading zone directly in front of the rec center and crowds of people hovered in little groupings. Heads turned their way and someone with a microphone followed by someone with a camera blocked their path.

Equal parts irritation, indignation, and protective instincts stiffened Molly's spine. Before the woman—who, according to the sticker on her mic, was from a station in a neighboring town—could speak, Molly held up her hand.

"We have no comment. And neither will anyone else."

"I'm just trying to do my job, Ms. Owens. Oh yes, I know *of* you. Her heartbroken fans are desperate to know: has Magnolia Sweet's final curtain closed?"

Molly didn't even try to stop the eye roll. She started to say more, but Sam pressed his hand to the small of her back and said in an unfriendly voice, "Excuse us, Miss. You're blocking our path."

He then slipped between Molly and his mother, an arm around both of their shoulders. He must have given a 'back off' vibe because no one else approached them.

She glanced toward her Jeep but Sam leaned down to whisper in her ear. "Chris will arrange to get it home. I gave him the keys."

They'd driven his mother's car, so while Katherine got in the driver's side, Sam slipped into the back with Molly.

"You could have ridden up front," she whispered, pulling the seatbelt over her lap.

He buckled his own and took her hand. "Indulge me a little and let me keep you close?"

She nodded and stared out the window as his mother drove them toward home. An unsettled, fluttery feeling took up residence in her chest and she rubbed at the pressure mounting there.

"You okay, Molly?" Katherine asked, catching her gaze in the rear-view mirror.

"Someone who truly believes in signs might think me constantly stumbling into things like this is a bad one," Molly said into the quiet of the car.

Sam's fingers tightened around her own but she couldn't look at him right now. Katherine took a right at the four way stop and Molly thought for a minute that maybe the woman hadn't heard her.

"So, you think maybe you're bad luck?" Katherine asked.

"Mom," Sam said more sharply than Molly had ever heard him speak to his mother before.

"Sam," Molly whispered, looking his way.

His scowl deepened when he looked at Molly. "That's garbage. You aren't bad luck."

They pulled into the driveway and Katherine cut the engine. She turned in her seat and smiled at them both. "Sam, honey. Why don't you go let Tigger out? Give me and your girl a minute."

Sam looked back and forth between the two women that Molly knew he loved fiercely. He clearly trusted them both as well, because he got out of the car and walked toward their cottage. Molly undid her seatbelt and shuffled forward.

"This is such a happy town," Molly whispered.

Katherine leaned her hand across the seat and Molly reached up to take it. "Honey, people die even in happy places. You know that. What on earth makes you think you're a catalyst for anything?"

She blinked back tears, the events of the night running through her brain like an old movie reel. "Chris was so irritated to see me tonight. He wasn't worried about me. It was like he just knew I'd be there. That's not exactly the thing a girl wants to be known for, right? Where there's death, there's got to be Molly."

Katherine squeezed her hand. "Sweet girl, you need to let the weight of Vernon's death go now. It was not your fault."

Molly swallowed the thickness in her throat. "I sent him on that interview."

"Yes, you did. But you did not kill him. You did not keep secrets and harbor them for years, pulling others into your tangled web. You didn't suggest he manipulate or blackmail anyone. You asked him to do his job."

She nodded. Logically, she knew this. But nothing felt very logical right now. "I've seen a lot of death since I got here."

"I know. But consider the other things that have happened since you arrived if you're really looking for a sign as to where you belong."

Molly's gaze locked on Katherine's. "What do you mean?"

"You saved *The Bulletin* from extinction. You helped Alan's family face a terrible demon. You've brought Hannah out of her shell. You know she asked if she could interview me the other day?" Katherine laughed. "That girl is a mini-you in the making. You helped bring closure to some sad circumstances, none of which are your fault. What would that bride and groom have done without you last summer? And perhaps, the most important, in my opinion, at least, you reminded my sweet, sensitive son that there's more to life than being under a car. You taught him to look up and start living again. You can't be a bad sign when I feel like you're his good luck charm."

Tears escaped and Molly swiped her cheek with the back of her hand. "Thank you."

"Thank *you*. Go on in and get some rest. I'll expect to see you both for breakfast tomorrow."

Molly got out of the car and gave Katherine a hard hug. As she walked down the lantern-lit path to her cottage, she smiled when she saw Sam leaning against the doorjamb, arms crossed.

"My mom talk some sense into you?" He opened his arms and she walked into them, tipping her head back so she could see his eyes in the moonlight.

"She thinks I'm your good luck charm," Molly whispered.

"She's not wrong," Sam said. As his head dipped lower and his lips brushed against her cheek, her jaw, along it to her ear, she felt a completely different kind of shiver wrack her body. "You're my everything."

His mouth closed over hers and some of the sadness seeped away. Sam's embrace, his touch, his whispered words reminded her that, as sad as Magnolia's death might be, she was very much alive.

The sound of whimpering that turned to deep barks broke them apart. Sam pressed his forehead to Molly's. "I think that's a *sign* that someone besides me missed you today."

Molly laughed and slipped her hand into Sam's. "We'd better let him in before he sends a signal to the entire neighborhood."

Chapter Seven

Molly woke before Sam, slipped quietly out of bed, and got ready for an early morning walk with Tigger. She turned the coffee on before she left the house, her mouth watering from the smell of the dark roast grounds.

Her thoughts were on overdrive this morning. The evening before played on repeat in her brain, one scene at a time. Some elusive string was tugging her attention and she didn't know what, exactly, was bothering her. Other than the obvious. When they crossed the road leading to the paths for the beach, Tigger tugged the leash toward the stairs.

"What's got you so excited?" She laughed when he looked back at her with eyes that seemed to say, *Come on, I'll show you.*

"Slow down," she said through a smile. It was like he could sense the pace of her brain. No wonder they got along so well.

Her phone buzzed in her pocket, so she forced Tigger to stop at the bottom. Sitting on one of the logs that looked toward the ocean, she pulled her phone out and checked the message.

Jill: You okay? Are the rumors true?

Molly had crashed on the couch when she'd gotten home, waking only to go to bed. Hardly professional, but obviously she'd needed the rest. She also realized that she needed to remove herself from the immediacy of what had happened. She was an editor rather than a reporter for a reason.

Molly: They are. I'm just walking Tigger. Meet me before work and we can talk?

Jill: You look good in that sweater. Is it Sam's?

Molly's head snapped up just as Tigger started to bark and shake his tail in absolute delight. Jill, dressed in running gear, blond hair pulled back into a high ponytail, approached them.

"You're out early this morning," Molly said, smiling at her friend.

Jill tucked the strand of hair blowing in her face behind her ear and laughed. "Well, I heard some rumors last night and followed up, but I didn't hear from you. I spoke to Alan after I read the entertainment news and updated the website. I had a hunch today would be busy. Thought I'd get my run in early. Plus, you bring Bella's goodies to all of us to assuage your own guilt."

Molly laughed, the sound rippling in the early morning breeze. "You're absolutely right about that. It's also why Tigger gets such frequent walks. And thank you. I should have updated you guys last night. I just…crashed."

"Don't apologize. I can't believe she's dead."

Tigger was running circles around their feet. Fortunately, Molly had dropped the leash, or she and Jill would be wound together like a duo from a farce. Her friend kneeled down and chuckled when Tigger bounced onto her thighs and tried to lick her face then immediately bounded to Molly, jumping up for attention.

"Oh, buddy. You're so sweet and happy. I'm telling you," Jill said, looking up at Molly, squinting against the sun. "If a man or a dog ever adore me the way yours adore you, I'm all in."

Molly kneeled down in the sand as well. "I am a lucky, lucky woman."

Jill finished giving Tigger rubs and stood up, dusting off her knees. "You deserve it. So? Tell me what's going on."

They walked along the beach, listening to waves roll alongside them, and Molly filled Jill in on what had happened yesterday. The beach was quiet this early in the morning, and while Molly never minded running into people she knew, she was glad.

"That's crazy. What do they think happened?" Jill asked, stopping to tie her running shoe.

"Given Chris's reaction to seeing me there, I'm guessing I won't be who he tells."

Jill stood up. "He's probably just stressed. I'm sure he didn't mean to make you feel bad."

Molly nodded. "I know. Just, since I came here, I've had more of a hands-on approach than I'd like. It's been necessary for the most part, but now I have you, Hannah, *and* Elizabeth. I need to go back to doing my job and gain a little more distance. It's hard in a town like this though. I've never experienced that before. The personal impact of what I'm reporting on, if that makes sense."

Jill gave a breathy laugh. "Trust me, it makes sense. This town is growing every day but I still know way too many people. If someone does something that we end up putting in the paper, chances are good I went to school with someone in their family, or their parent taught me, or some other weird connection."

Molly snapped her fingers as they took the path up the bank that led to the parking lot. "Exactly. It's more than just news on a page."

Jill and Molly both stopped at the top of the incline and Tigger flopped across Molly's feet.

"That can be a blessing and a curse. You *do* have us on board now though, and as a single, dog-free woman who spends most evenings watching television or playing a word game against strangers online, let me step up. I'll go shower and head over to the station, do follow-up interviews at the theater and see what's happening with the production."

Molly nodded her agreement. "That's perfect. I met a writer the other night and he emailed me some samples. I'll get on finding someone to hire while you do that. But since, you know, you're the one out and about..."

Jill glanced across the street at Morning Muffins before meeting Molly's gaze. She laughed and nodded. "I'll bring treats."

"We *did* just exercise," Molly pointed out.

"This is why you're in charge. All that wisdom."

Molly laughed and waved to her friend, heading toward home more settled and clearheaded. Tigger trotted along as the town woke up. He turned his head from side to side, dropping it to sniff any new scent he caught, then started over.

Routine was good. She'd always been a fan of it. Since she'd arrived at the beginning of June the year before, hers had been in flux. If they could get another solid, reliable hire or two at *The Bulletin*, it would go a long way toward making things run smoother.

As she walked along the quiet streets, she breathed in the slightly salty air, making a list of what she needed to do for the day. Her brain tried a few times to shift back to the scene from the evening before, but Molly forced her mind back on track. By the time she got back to the cottage, Sam was up, dressed, and drinking his coffee at the island countertop.

Tigger ran to him like they'd been apart for dog years, making Sam's deep chuckle fill the small space. Yes, she was a lucky, lucky woman. Sam rubbed Tigger's exposed belly and then stood and greeted Molly, pulling her in for a hug. When he'd squeezed her tight, he leaned away and captured her face between his hands.

"Good walk? Your cheeks are all rosy," he said, brushing his nose along the bridge of hers.

"Mmm. It was great. Quiet. I ran into Jill."

Sam chuckled, pressing a quick kiss to her lips. "Then it wasn't quiet. My cousin never stops talking."

Molly swatted him and then went to grab a mug for coffee. "That's not true. She's delightful."

Sam sat down at the island again, grinning at her as he picked up his coffee. "Sure. She's delightful. Tell me why, when we were growing up, she used to hide my aunt's keys every time we got together so she wouldn't have to leave, and then always blamed me?"

Molly couldn't help the laughter that erupted. She poured her coffee, saying, "See? Delightful and clever."

Sam shook his head, but she caught the hint of his smile before he drank. When he set his mug down again, his smile had faded. "You check the news this morning?"

She shook her head and took her own blessed sip of morning clarity. She didn't even try to hide her enjoyment. When she set her mug down, she grabbed some bread to make toast. "Nope. I was up early and just wanted to get Tigger out."

"I would have gone with you," Sam said.

"I know. But you looked so peaceful."

"There's a lot of chatter on social media about Magnolia."

Molly's pulse blipped. They were a news outlet and it was their job to report, to share, to work the stories. And they were behind. "Jill mentioned it. She's following up with Chris right now. I figured he could use a break from me asking him questions."

"Chris just worries about you, babe. You two are kind of connected in multiple ways." Sam leaned on his forearms, watching her as she waited for her toast.

"What do you mean?"

"He's always had a protective streak toward his friends and family. It's who he is. Then you add in the cop so it ups that factor. Pile on you being the significant other of his best friend in addition to a friend of the woman he cares for? That's a lot of responsibility he feels toward you."

Molly bit her lip, trying not to grin like a fool. Sam, of course, noticed. "What has you looking like I just threw sunshine at you?"

She laughed and met his gaze, her heart feeling suspiciously mushy. He was taking away her jaded edge with all his sweetness. "Significant other sounds so serious." *Dork. You're such a huge dork.* But she couldn't contain the smile.

Sam laughed and came around the counter. He took her arms and pulled her up to her toes, bringing their faces nose-to-nose. "I'm sort of serious about you, if you haven't figured it out yet, Ms. Owens."

Molly pushed up further and wrapped her arms around his neck. "My observation skills are very keen so I did, in fact, notice. Every now and again though, I get a little reminder that this—*you*—are real and it sends a little thrill through me all over again. I feel very grateful."

Rubbing his hands up her arms and down her back, he pressed his lips to the spot just under her jaw and dragged them up to her ear. "It's real. I'm real. It goes both ways."

Sam's mouth found hers and she pushed everything else away. When he kissed her like that, nothing else existed. Her toast popped, startling them apart.

Giving her one more kiss on her forehead, he backed away. "I need to get to work. I'm picking up my mom's gift after but I'll see you tonight."

"You absolutely will."

He stared at her, his gaze dark, heated, and intense. "I love you."

Molly's heart pumped an extra beat with the thrill of those words. "I love you back."

* * * *

Only Elizabeth was at *The Bulletin* when Molly arrived. She was at her own desk, closest to the street entrance, working on her laptop.

"Hi!" Elizabeth got up immediately and followed Molly into her office.

"Hi. I take it you've heard about Magnolia." Molly stowed her jacket and purse on the standing coat rack in the corner of her office and then went to her desk.

"I can't believe it. I was talking to Deb Connors. She's in the play, her and her boyfriend, Beau. The police interviewed everyone last night, but apparently the station phoned and asked them both to come in this morning, too."

Molly frowned as she opened up her own laptop. "They probably just want to follow up on something. Things were...chaotic last night." It did seem strange to do second interviews again the next day. Unless they were suspects, there was no reason...Molly sat up straighter. "Did she say whether foul play was suspected?" Jill or Sam would have said if they'd read that online.

Elizabeth sat down, leaning forward. "No. She mostly talked about how mad she was over how hard her boyfriend was taking it. She lives in the same complex as Magnolia, and I guess there's been heaps of tension."

None of this made any sense. It was no secret Magnolia Sweet wasn't a friendly person. It was very likely that where she went, tension followed. "But if one of the props fell on her and caused her death, why would the police need to talk to them again? Her death was an accident."

It would seem so but Molly couldn't shake the convenience of how she was lying under the house. Like she'd been…positioned.

The front door chimes jingled and a moment later, Jill sailed into Molly's office. Her hair was pulled into a tight, styled bun and she'd clearly showered and changed for work. "Are we talking about Magnolia?"

"Of course," Elizabeth said. "I didn't know the woman and I'm sorry she died but I can't help but be intrigued by the amount of drama that she's still managing to create. I was just telling Molly about my friend Deb. Well, friend in the loosest sense of the word. We play cards together sometimes."

Jill pulled off her jacket and purse, hanging them alongside Molly's. "Deb Connors. Auntie Em, correct?"

Elizabeth nodded. "She is. Do you know if the play is still moving forward?"

Molly leaned back, watching her friend closely. She was keyed up for sure. She knew something and was dying to share it.

"I know many things, my dear Elizabeth," Jill said. She sat down in the second chair in front of Molly's desk. "Including the fact that Magnolia Sweet did not die accidentally. She was killed."

Molly leaned forward. "How? She didn't have a mark on her."

"I'm guessing you couldn't see her neck? Turns out, she was strangled."

Chapter Eight

Jill took advantage of their open-mouthed shock to fill them in on what she'd found. Popping up from her seat, like she couldn't contain her energy, she paced the small space.

"I went to ask a couple of follow-up questions at the station and Priscilla was on the desk," Jill said.

That was hardly surprising since Priscilla, a mutual friend, worked there full time. In Molly's experience, however, she was very professional and rarely prone to divulging even the smallest of details unless she'd drank too much. And that had only happened once.

"I was asking to see Detective Beatty—it's so weird to call the boy who used to help my cousin shove wet sand in my shoes that—but he was walking out of the back when I arrived. When I told him why I was there, he gave me a stock statement."

She hurried over to her jacket and pulled her phone from the pocket, pulling something up on the screen. "Magnolia Sweet's cause of death is yet to be determined but after further investigation, we do suspect foul play. We do not believe the community is in any danger but if anyone has any information regarding Ms. Sweet in the hours before her death that they feel would add value to our ongoing investigation…then he gave me the station tip number."

Molly shook her head, trying to absorb the fact that she had been standing at the scene of another crime.

"They didn't say strangled," Elizabeth noted, turning in her seat to follow Jill's movements.

Jill came and sat down again. "No. Because that's how they weed out the calls. When Chris walked away, Priscilla made a comment about how she'd be answering the phone non-stop for days now—she helps out on the tip line when she's not working the front desk."

"So does Hannah," Molly said, thinking about the possible overlap and scheduling difficulties.

Jill nodded and waved her hand dismissively. "Worry about that later. So anyway, I asked her how she'd weed out the calls to know if anything is helpful."

Molly smiled. "Nicely done. As if you don't already know." They received similar phone calls at *The Bulletin* from people who wanted to share information, ranging from concerned citizens to conspiracy theorists.

Jill sat up straighter, tossing her long, straight, blonde hair over one shoulder dramatically. "Right? She whisper told me that Magnolia had been strangled and *arranged* that way on purpose."

"Like what on purpose?" Elizabeth asked.

Molly swallowed around the thickness in her throat. "Like the Wicked Witch of the East."

Jill's smile faded and she leaned forward, reached out for Molly's hand. "Hey. You okay? Sorry. I'm being all bubbly about this because it's solid news, but I forgot for a minute that you had to see it."

Molly shook her head, breathed through her nose. "I'm fine. I'm also positive Chris wouldn't be okay with those details being printed."

"No. Priscilla threatened bodily harm and mentioned her access to tasers and pepper spray."

Molly and Elizabeth laughed but the tension didn't ease all the way out of Molly's shoulders. The images she'd pushed out of her mind came rushing forward again, with new and startling clarity. Instead of strings tugging in the back of her mind, it was more like tug-of-war rope being yanked from both ends.

* * * *

Not your problem. Not your problem. Not your problem. No, Molly's *problem* was that now she couldn't stop remembering little details that she shouldn't be thinking about. As she waited to cross Main Street at the end of it, where they'd installed a crosswalk by *The Bulletin* building, she couldn't stop thinking about what she'd seen in a new light.

Who would kill her? The image of Judd crouched over the body came back with alarming clarity. When she'd arrived, her heart had dropped to her feet. The shock had forced her backward, but the ravaged look on

Judd's face had eased the unspoken worry that it was him. Then he'd saved her immediately after.

The little bird chirp signalling she could cross sounded and Molly waved at the driver of a car stopped at the light. She didn't know him, but it was automatic now. Everyone in Britton Bay waved at everyone. Across the street were more shops with false and real fronts that resembled an Old-World town with a modern update. She loved it here. She loved the pretty colors on the buildings and the way the lower half of most of them were aged brick. She also loved that her boyfriend's auto shop was across the street and just up from Come N' Get it Café so they could meet and go for lunch.

A lot of the shops on Sam's side were eateries, but there was also his auto shop, an empty storefront, a vintage goods store, and a small bookstore and card shop. There wasn't much a person couldn't get on Main Street.

As she neared Sam's garage, she smiled at the exterior. He worked so hard to make it successful. Only one story, his building was square, white-washed concrete. The front building had an office and sales center. There was a secondary larger building in the back with bays for working on cars. Molly stopped and looked up at the rounded, slowly moving sign that read "Sam's Auto Shop."

He'd bought the place with the money his father had bequeathed to him and put his all into doing what he loved but also thought would make his father proud.

"Hey there," Sam said, coming out of the building. He was dressed in jeans and a t-shirt and Molly shivered just looking at him, happy she wore a sweater.

Spring was here but the sun still hid behind fluffy white clouds and the sky couldn't make up its mind as to whether or not it wanted to rain.

"Hey, yourself." Molly put her hands on his chest as his came to her waist and went up on tiptoe. He met her halfway, kissing her with a sweetness that dulled the noise in her brain.

When she pulled away from the kiss, she slipped her arms further around his neck and held on.

"You okay?" He whispered the words against her hair, making her smile.

"I am. I just like being close to you."

"Back at you."

She dropped to her flat feet and they strolled, hand-in-hand, down the block toward the restaurant. Sam swung their arms between them as they stopped and checked out the barrels along the way.

"You should do one in the shape of a car," Molly said, tipping her head back to look up at him. She squinted against the sun.

"Too late now but that's a good idea. Maybe next year. You could help me."

Her heart gave the usual lurch that came with Sam's mentions of the future. Of his absolute conviction that they were meant to be. She loved it. She definitely felt the same toward him but after a life of moving around, it still felt strange to have someone feel so…tied to her.

He held the door open for her, the bell giving a little jingle. The Come N' Get It was busy, but not like it was during the lunch rushes of summer. It was beginning, though. Here and there, people trickled into and out of the town, staying for a night or two, maybe a week. As summer came closer, the shops and streets would get busier.

"Come on in, you two," Calli called from the back of the restaurant, where she was picking up an order. "There's a booth back here. Give me two secs and I'll wipe it down for you."

Sam grinned down at Molly. "The service in this town is fantastic."

Molly laughed. "Especially when you hang out with the guy everyone has a soft spot for."

When they slid into the booth, Sam was still smiling. "As long as you do."

Calli came over with a spray bottle and cloth and wiped down the tabletop.

"Hey cuties. You doing okay, Molly? Heard you stumbled onto a terrible scene."

It was no surprise that Calli knew, but Molly just didn't want to talk about it right now. There were too many mixed emotions swimming around inside of her.

"Yeah. It was pretty awful."

Calli squeezed her shoulder. "Let's get you fixed up with some comfort food. What can I get you today?" She swiped a strand of hair out of her face with the back of her hand.

They knew the menu well enough not to need it. Molly didn't need any time to decide. "I'll have a cola and the battered chicken tacos."

"I'll have a root beer float and the Bay Burger with fries."

"You want two straws for that float?" Calli waggled her eyebrows at them. Molly laughed. "I'll stick to my cola."

Making a tutting sound, she waved her index finger at them. "Just because you live together now doesn't mean you can't still be romantic."

Sam chuckled, leaning back in the booth with one arm stretched out. Molly's eyes wandered over him appreciatively but she kept it to herself that she had no problem being romantic with Sam.

"I think we're managing to keep the magic alive, Calli. Try not to worry," Sam said.

Her face cleared of all humor. "Give me a minute to put your order in and then I'd actually like to talk to you, Molly, about something I *am* worried about."

She moved away, stopping at another table and chatting with them a moment.

"What do you think that's about?" Sam asked.

"I have no idea." She shrugged her shoulders.

"I read on Twitter that Magnolia was murdered," Sam said quietly, shifting and putting both arms on the table, leaning into their conversation.

She'd popped online to see the updates before she'd left *The Bulletin*. Jill was taking over their social media accounts and website. She'd printed Chris's statement and gave a little background on Magnolia and the play.

"That's the story. I'm letting Jill take full rein. I heard back from Gavin. He emailed with some of his writing samples and I ran them past Alan. We're going to give him a few freelance jobs first, see how he does. I'm putting my focus there and on editing."

"So, no sleuthing?" One side of his mouth tipped up. His tone held no censure even though she knew she'd scared him more than once with her curious ways.

"Nope. That's what Chris is for. I'm staying out of it." She was still stung that Chris had just naturally expected her to be where she shouldn't.

"Babe, I'm positive he didn't mean to hurt your feelings."

Molly shrugged again. Sam reached for her hand. "I'll still beat him up for you though. If you want."

Her smile stretched and she squeezed his fingers. "I love that you would but there's no need. It's fine. Everything is fine. I just need to do the job I came here to do, and with all of the things that have happened it's taken a back seat. *The Bulletin* needs more staff. Sooner rather than later. Especially with this news. Hannah's been helping out at the station, and with a tip line open for the investigation, she might end up being there more than the paper."

"Hmm. There's got to be people looking for work. Does Jill know anyone?"

Molly nodded but didn't answer since Calli came back over with three drinks on a tray. She set Molly and Sam's in front of them and picked up the third, giving the tray to one of the servers walking by. She slid into the booth beside Molly.

"I'm joining you for a minute," Calli said, taking a long sip of her own cola.

"Calli, I don't pay you to bug the customers," Dean called out with a laugh.

"Oh yes you do," she hollered back.

Sam waved to Dean. Molly turned her head and did the same.

"Never mind him. We've got a problem," Calli said.

"We as in the three of us?" Sam asked, not even attempting to hide his amusement.

Calli shook her head. "We as in the citizens of Britton Bay. One of us is missing."

Chapter Nine

Molly caught Sam's frown before she turned her body on the bench to better face Calli.

"Who's missing?"

"Corky." Calli ran her fingers up and down her soda glass absently.

"Now Calli, he never stays in one spot long." Sam patted her hand.

Corky Templeton was a homeless man who lived on the streets of Britton Bay. He'd been around so long that no one could really remember when he'd first appeared. He didn't seem to have family in the area but the residents of the town took care of him however they could. He typically refused to stay at the local shelter just outside of town unless the weather was beyond survivable. Merchants and townsfolk alike treated him to food and beverages but Corky didn't ask for anything. If he was in an okay mood he'd chat your ear off, but if he was wound up he'd try his best to convince a person someone was after him.

"Why do you think he's missing, Calli?" Molly asked as a couple of patrons came in, the bell jingling at their arrival.

"He hasn't been in here in over two weeks. He comes every morning for coffee. Coffee here, day-old muffins from Bella—he won't take the fresh ones. I know he wanders and he's gone days in a row before without showing his face. But I can feel it in my bones. Something isn't right."

Dean appeared at their side. He put a basket of homemade chips on the table.

He shook Sam's hand and gave Molly a wave. "What's not right is pulling people into your conspiracy theory. He's fine, Calli. As much as we think we know him, we don't know if he drinks or does drugs. Could be he's off doing that. You can't be everyone's mother." Dean put his hand on his wife's shoulder and squeezed, looking at her with affection and concern.

Calli shook her head. "Something isn't right."

"Have you talked to Chris?" Sam asked.

Molly was trying to remember the last time she'd seen Corky. Not in a while. He usually wandered around town. He cleaned up the community garden by the park, collected bottles, and hung out at the pier. But Molly hadn't seen him anywhere in longer than she could remember.

"Chris said he'd keep an eye out and tell his patrol guys to do the same, but there's no one who can really report him missing, right?"

"No. Probably not. But maybe we could do a notice in *The Bulletin*. Just make more citizens aware that he hasn't been seen in a while."

The bell rang from the kitchen, pulling Dean's focus. "That'd probably put her mind to rest, Molly. Well, on that subject at least."

That brought a small smile. Dean went back to the kitchen and Calli got up from the table. "It would. That would be great, Molly. I just…he's one of us, you know?"

Molly smiled at the woman whose heart was as bright as her smile. "I do. I'll get something on the website today."

Picking up her soda glass, she straightened her shoulders and put her smile back on. "Let me go grab your lunches."

Molly smiled after her, turning her head to see Sam looking at her. "What?"

He shook his head, a gentle laugh escaping his lips. "Nothing. I just like how invested you are in everything."

"She's not wrong. He is one of us," Molly said as Calli approached again.

"He is. And so are you."

Calli dropped off their meals. Molly dug into hers with gusto. She was hungrier than she'd realized. She and Sam talked about the upcoming summer season and the idea of getting away together for a few days. They talked about finishing up the back deck and sitting on it under the summer stars. Molly's heart was wrapped up in both of those things. But her brain was having a hard time staying focused. She kept thinking about Corky and Magnolia, and how nothing was ever as simple as it seemed.

* * * *

Molly spent the day going over Jill and Elizabeth's stories, making tweaks and changes before working on the layout pages for the next edition. The newspaper went out on Thursday mornings and most of the week was focused on getting everything ready for a Wednesday afternoon printing. Since today was Wednesday, they needed to make sure all of the content was ready to go. It still thrilled Molly that there was an actual printing press in the basement of *The Bulletin*. She loved going down there and inhaling the scent of the ink and listening to the sound of the papers whipping through the machine. They could have had the paper sent out, but Alan was a traditionalist at heart. They would likely have to digitize by upgrading their machine, but for now she liked the old-school nature of it.

With the layout set to go—Alan would do the printing—Molly was wrapping up her day and getting ready to go home. She pulled up the paper's Facebook page and scanned the comments to her post.

She'd found an old picture of Corky and posted:

Corky Templeton hasn't been seen in his usual hangouts for a while. If you've seen or spoken to him lately, please comment below. Several concerned citizens have mentioned his absence.

There were already over fifty comments. Molly read through them and decided, based on what people said, that it had been at least a week since he'd last been spotted. She hated the thought of him out there on his own. Others had tried to help him, bringing him into the shelter, even offering him a place to stay, but he was proud. Molly pulled out her journal and made a note to do some digging on Corky's family. Maybe it was time to see if he had any roots in the area or if he'd just landed here like she had.

She closed her laptop, ready to lock up because the others had gone home and Alan was in the basement. But Jill came rushing through the back door of the building just as Molly was double checking the small kitchenette they all used to ensure it was tidy.

"Hey. What are you doing back here?" Molly asked, loading a couple of mugs into the dishwasher.

Jill shook off her hair, letting Molly know the rain had started again. Removing her jacket, her breath coming in and out in short bursts, she walked over to Molly.

"They've made an arrest," Jill said, the words rushing out of her in an unusually high octave.

Molly reared back. "What?"

"They arrested someone for the murder of Magnolia Sweet." Jill rubbed her hands together, probably to warm them.

"How? It's only been a day. Who is it?" Her thoughts tumbled. Judd, over the body. Someone who looked like Tiffany, leaving. The silence of the auditorium. The busy parking lot. Had she walked right past a murderer?

"All their evidence points to one person. I'm not entirely sure yet what it is but I was leaving the station when I heard who they were heading out to arrest."

Molly's nerves were stretching thin. "Tell me. Who is it? Do we know them?"

"You might not. But a lot of us do. It's Judd Brown. Our old school janitor."

Chapter Ten

Molly had to turn all alerts connected to *The Bulletin* off on her phone by noon the next day. Chewing the end of a pen, she walked to the window and looked out at the rain. It was coming down hard, drenching the streets and making the world, in general, gloomy.

The mood in the office wasn't much better and Molly didn't know how to help anyone. Jill had run the online story first thing this morning. The white cloth beneath Magnolia's head had been a monogrammed handkerchief. Judd had been holding one just like it when Molly saw him at the theater. Her stomach twisted with the memory.

In addition to that, texts between Magnolia and Judd had given the police all of the evidence they apparently needed to make an arrest. In a regular situation, the town would be thrilled to see a murder investigation wrapped up so quickly. If Molly were truly on the outside looking in, she'd be commending the Britton Bay Police Department for their quick and diligent work.

"I'm going to head down to Bella's," Jill said behind Molly.

Molly turned, lowering the pen. "In this rain?"

Jill's typically happy eyes were red-rimmed. "I'm hungry and need a break."

"You can go home," Molly said, crossing the room to her friend.

Jill shrugged. Molly pulled her in for a hug and held on tight. The community as a whole was shocked by Judd Brown's arrest. Shocked and outraged. Hence, muting the alerts.

"Go home, Jill. We're fine here," Molly whispered.

"I'm sorry." Jill stepped away and sniffled.

"Don't be sorry. He matters to you."

Jill pulled her bottom lip between her teeth and worried it for a moment before letting out a watery laugh. "When we were in ninth grade, my friend and I found a little family of possums at the back of the field. A few of the boys were being jerks and trying to scare them. I ran into Judd in the hallway on the way to class. I was upset and he asked what was wrong. That afternoon, when school let out, he got me and my friend to show him where they were. He brought a box and coaxed them in, took them to the animal shelter in the next town."

Molly's heart ached for Jill. And for Sam, who'd been equally shocked and saddened to read the news.

"I don't know what to say. Sometimes we think we know a person, but maybe we never really do. Not all the way through." She'd seen enough in the last six months to know that even 'good' people had a snapping point. "Go home. Work on the photos for the barrel challenge. The voting starts next week. But only if you're up to it."

Jill nodded. "Okay. Thanks."

Molly gave her another hug and went to make some coffee once she left. Elizabeth was working on the online voting pages for the contest next week. People would be able to browse through the photographs and summaries of the barrels and cast their votes. Alan had stayed home with his wife. Gavin was set to come in that afternoon, so Molly would be on her own for a while. Hannah was also set to come in after school.

Letting out a heavy sigh, Molly wished she'd brought Tigger for company today. As the weather got better, she'd start doing it more. Once her coffee was ready, she wandered back through the opening that separated the staffroom, kitchen, and storage area of the building from the front.

On her way into her office, she glanced out the window again, just in time to see someone come through the door. It wasn't completely uncommon, having people stop by to say hello, place an ad, or share a story. But Molly didn't recognize the woman closing her umbrella and shaking off the water. Her long, bold, red nails blazed against the dark, damp material.

Dressed in a long black trench coat and heels that would land Molly on her face in seconds, the woman straightened, tossing her very blond hair behind her shoulder.

"Hi," she said, stepping forward, almost cautiously, like she wasn't sure she was in the right place. Despite the near-monsoon happening outside, the woman's makeup was flawless. Smokey shadow highlighted her brown eyes, and whether it was contouring or good genes, she had a striking jaw line.

"Hi." Molly stepped forward, her coffee in one hand, her other ready to introduce herself.

"I'm Vivien Sweet."

Walking closer, Molly reached out to shake her hand. "I'm Molly Owens." She schooled her features and did her best to stop the questions racing through her mind. "You're Magnolia's daughter?"

Vivien nodded. "Yes."

"I'm so sorry about your mother," Molly said. Regardless of the rumors she'd heard about Magnolia not being close to her children, it had to be awful to lose a parent.

"Thank you. My brother Jeffrey was supposed to meet me here but I think he's running behind," Vivien said, looking around the space, her eyes stopping on the multiple framed newspapers that lined the wall.

"Is there something I can help you with?" Molly set her coffee down on Elizabeth's desk.

Setting her closed umbrella down in one of the chairs, Vivien opened her large black handbag and pulled out an envelope, handing it to Molly.

"We'd like to run a full-page ad for my mother. There are details regarding the funeral and paying respects. Despite the fact that she wasn't well liked, the vultures will want to know."

Molly grimaced. Vivien wasn't wrong. If anything, there'd be more interest in her mother's death because of the controversy around it. People were filling *The Bulletin's* feed with stories they remembered of Magnolia's time in Britton Bay, along with things about Judd.

Molly accepted the envelope. "If the funeral is before next Thursday, we can run it online, but our next edition isn't until then."

"It's next Saturday," Vivien said. She closed her handbag and picked up her umbrella. "The play opens the next night so the timing works well."

Molly didn't quite understand what that meant, but was surprised to hear the play was still happening. "They're going forward with it?"

Standing straighter and tipping her chin up just a little, she gave a smile that made Molly think of Magnolia. "Of course. My mother would be horrified if they didn't. Haven't you heard? The show must go on."

Okay, sure, Molly thought, *if a cast member quits or gets sick or even breaks a literal leg. But surely not when the director is murdered? On set?*

"It's what she would have wanted," Vivien said quietly, obviously reading Molly's face.

"Then I'm glad they're doing it." She didn't have to know or like the woman to feel sadness over the way her life ended. The quiet that settled between them threw Molly off. What was there to say? "Uh, the set looked amazing."

Vivien arched both brows. "I'm sure it did."

"You haven't seen it?" Molly wanted to smack herself. What was wrong with her? Of course, the woman hadn't seen it. Why would she go to the place her mother was murdered? Though Molly wasn't sure she'd be able to stay away if something happened to her own mom. She'd need to know every piece of information she could.

The daughter's laugh was somewhat chilling. "We just arrived last night. Even if we hadn't, my brother and I stopped going to anything my mother directed or produced before the opening over twenty years ago. She claimed we were bad luck."

The small gasp escaped her lungs before she could stop it. "I'm sorry." Making a mental note to call her mother and thank her for being a wonderful human being, Molly pasted a tight smile on her face. "Is there anything else I can do?"

Vivien looked like she wanted to say something—her mouth opening, then closing—but only shook her head.

"Well, let me know if there is." Molly tucked her hands in the pockets of her jeans.

"Thank you."

Vivien turned on her heels and left. Molly watched her through the picture window. She hadn't noticed the long, sleek, black limo parked outside. A driver held the door open and she slid in. Glancing down at the envelope, Molly picked up her coffee and took both items to her office.

The obituary that Vivien had given Molly was long and detailed, highlighting her mother's great triumphs and successes. Everything in it focused on her career and said nothing about her being missed or whom she'd left behind. Molly couldn't believe her eyes when she read the last line:

Whether you cared for our mother or not, we encourage you to come together as a community—one she was happy to be a part of—and show your kindness by attending the play she poured her heart, soul, and last days into.

It was unlike any announcement Molly had ever read. It didn't mention Jeffrey or Vivien or anything about Magnolia as a *person.* Only as an actress. *Maybe that's all she was, even to them.* Molly felt guilty for the thought, but the evidence of it was in her hand.

She worked through the afternoon, pleased to hear the bell over the door signal company. Laughter flitted into her office, letting her know Hannah had come in with someone. Getting up, Molly stretched and pulled in a deep breath. She'd been hunched over her laptop for hours.

A smile was already on her face, and it grew when she saw Bella with a take-out box, chatting with Hannah. At almost eighteen, Hannah was both a typical all-American girl with her long blond hair pulled up into one of those ballet buns, and a young woman on the cusp of adulthood. Bella was a couple of inches shorter than the senior and at least ten years older, but had her brown hair pulled up in a similar fashion. Molly had given it a try once, but she'd looked like she'd attached a dust rag to her head.

"Hey, two of my favorite people," Molly said, joining them. "What's that?"

Bella laughed and handed over the pale pink box. "Gloomy day reinforcements in the form of a new recipe I tried."

Molly opened the box and looked at the delicious looking tartlets. She grinned at her friend and pulled some out, offering one to Hannah, who accepted, and Bella, who passed. Setting down the box, she removed the dessert from its tin casing and checked it out.

"It's graham cracker, peanut butter, and chocolate ganache. I haven't named it yet," Bella said, her voice low and, if Molly was guessing right, a little nervous.

Molly and Hannah both took a bite. Molly closed her eyes and sighed around the delicious blend of peanut butter, chocolate, and the little crunch of crust. Hannah made a loud "mmm" sound.

Molly opened her eyes and pinned them on Bella. Before she took another bite, she suggested, "How about Heaven? Pure Deliciousness? Peanut Butter Perfection?"

Bella laughed.

"Oh my gosh, this is wicked good, Bella," Hannah said, taking another huge bite that almost finished it off.

"Yay. I'm so glad you guys like it."

"Love. Love it," Molly corrected, finishing hers. "What inspired you?"

Bella's smile faded and she made herself busy, closing the top of the box and straightening it on the desk. "Oh, just not sleeping. You know how it is."

Molly and Hannah exchanged a glance. They knew how it was for Bella dating Callan, who didn't always treat her the way she deserved.

Stepping back and pasting a bright smile on her face, Bella clapped her hands together. "I need to get going. Hey, we should do another girls' night at Sarah's."

Sarah held art classes and art evenings at her small studio. Bella, Hannah, Molly, and several other friends, including Sam's mom, had gotten together to try their hands at painting. Molly was better at typing, but it had been fun.

"I'd love to do that," Hannah said.

Bella poked her in the shoulder. "Shouldn't you be hanging out with kids your age rather than old ladies like us?"

Molly laughed, debating whether or not to have another tartlet. "Ouch."

"You guys are way more fun than high school girls. Besides, I really like Naomi," Hannah said, referring to Sarah's assistant. "Oh, speaking of which, I meant to text you." She looked at Molly.

"About?"

"Naomi went back to the shelter the other day to say hi to a couple friends she'd made there. She's pretty sure she saw Corky walking along the side of the road."

"Oh," Molly said, digesting the information. The homeless population in the small coastal town was higher than it should have been. It was a problem the town acknowledged but didn't know quite how to deal with. Several of the displaced people had opted against getting the help they needed, whether it was a place to stay or something more.

"Okay. Thanks. I'll see if I can follow up on that somehow," Molly said.

"Poor guy. I hope he's okay," Bella said as Gavin swept into the building, holding a black backpack over his head and hunched shoulders.

He lowered it and smiled at all three women. "Hey there. It's miserable out."

Molly was about to reply when she saw Bella's eyes widen and rake over Gavin in a very appreciative way. Biting back her grin, Molly stepped forward, holding a hand out to welcome him.

"Thanks for braving it. Come on in. Ladies, this is Gavin Bright. He's a freelance writer who is going to work with us. Gavin, this is Bella, owner of Morning Muffins, the bakery a few doors down. And this is Hannah Benedict, our social media guru and writer."

Gavin shook their hands. Maybe it was Molly's romantic imagination, but she thought he held Bella's a few seconds longer as they locked gazes.

Bella pulled back, smiling very widely and looking around like she'd forgotten something. "Well, okay. I should, go. I should get going."

Molly stifled her laugh. "See you later."

She turned then turned back and waved. "Nice to meet you."

Gavin gave a little wave, wiping some damp dark hair off his forehead. "You, too, Bella."

Despite being a teenager, Hannah schooled her features better than Molly and just grinned behind Gavin's back, giving a less than subtle nod. "Guess I'll get to work."

"And I'll get you settled, Gavin. Let me show you around."

As Molly walked him through the office, she wondered how things could feel both so hopeful and so desolate. New beginnings on the heels of sad endings. Life was such a double-edged sword and sometimes that was hard to truly wrap her head around. It made her want to grab onto the good and hang on tight. Which was exactly what she planned to do when she headed home to Sam that night.

Chapter Eleven

The rain had stopped by the time Molly pulled her Jeep into the driveway behind the bed and breakfast. When she slipped out of the vehicle, laptop bag and purse slung over her shoulder, she took a minute to breathe in the mingling scents of ocean air and flowers. The grass and petals had droplets clinging to them, and she was glad there was a small cobbled walkway that led from her parking area to the cottage so her shoes wouldn't get wet.

The sun was doing its best to peek through the clouds. If the sky continued to clear up, they might be able to see the moon and stars from their almost-finished deck later that night. Letting herself into their home, she slipped off her shoes, grinning at the sound of Sam singing along with the country radio station and Tigger doing his doggy best to out-wail him.

Setting her laptop and purse down on the entry table, she padded into the kitchen, biting her lip to keep from giggling. Sam was stirring something delicious-smelling on the stove and Tigger was on his back, feet in the air, crooning. There was no other word for it, and laughter burst from her lips. Tigger did some sort of fast reverse turtle maneuver and galloped over to her. Sam's cheeks darkened slightly, but his smile was no less infectious than Tigger's happiness.

"Didn't hear you come in," he said, turning the burner down as Molly crouched to rub Tigger.

"Not surprising, Luke Bryan. It's a good thing you two are so cute," she said, standing to greet him with a hug and a kiss.

He pulled her close, picking her up off her feet, burying his face in her hair.

"I already knew you didn't fall in love with me for my singing," he said, setting her down.

She put both of her hands to his face and went up on tiptoe. "I love everything about you. Horrible singing and all."

He laughed and tugged on a strand of her hair. "Cute. How was your day?"

Tigger had collapsed on her feet, and she felt bad shuffling him off so she could pour herself a glass of wine. Sam had a beer open on the counter, but she had noted the yummy smells were of the spaghetti sauce variety and decided wine would suit better.

"It was okay. Gloomy. I'll be glad when the weather gets better more consistently. How was yours? You seem like you're doing a bit better."

Sam grabbed a pot from one of the cupboards and started filling it with water for the pasta. "You mean about Judd? I still can't wrap my head around it. I know you never really know what's going on inside of someone's head but there's nothing about him that says killer to me. I just don't get it. The fund-raising page his cousin started and seeing how the town is rallying made me feel better though."

Molly paused as she was slipping the wine back in the fridge. "What?" She was starting to think she was losing her touch. Uncovering stories was her *thing.* But she was getting distracted, being pulled in too many directions: Corky, the murder, the play, firing Clay, Katherine's party, worrying about Bella and Callan, hiring Gavin, wondering about the chemistry between Gavin and Bella. *Too many things. Pick a road, Owens.*

She gathered plates and utensils, setting them at the island countertop where they ate as Sam filled her in.

"His cousin Tripp started a Facebook page to put up the money for Judd's release. No one wants him sitting in jail while he waits for a hearing. His bail was set this afternoon and by six, they'd raised double the money."

"What will the rest go towards?"

Sam set their plates in front of them and joined her at the island. "Living expenses. He'll likely be suspended from his job indefinitely."

Molly's heart cracked a little, but she reminded herself that Chris had proof—reason to arrest this man—and though others might see him in a certain light, clearly there was something they didn't know.

"I'm glad that the community is banding together for him. I met Magnolia's daughter today. Very polished, aloof, a little sad, but sort of cold. It was strange. She and her brother want to run a full-page homage to their mom in the next edition."

"I can't imagine being that disconnected from my mom."

"Me neither." Molly pulled off a chunk of garlic bread.

They ate in silence for a few minutes, and Molly remembered that she had wanted to phone her parents tonight. Just to touch base and remind them how grateful she was.

"You okay?" Sam rubbed his hand up and down her back, making her arch into the motion.

"Better when you do that," she said with a smile.

He leaned over, pressing his lips to her forehead. Because she could, she slipped off her stool and between his legs, wrapping her arms around his waist. He pulled her close.

"In case I haven't said it recently, you're pretty awesome," she said, pressing her mouth to the warm skin on his neck.

His hands moved up and down, easing the strain of the day out of her muscles. "Hmm. I'm glad you think so."

Leaning back a bit, he brought his hands to her face and stared at Molly. Those eyes, that gaze. She'd fallen for them immediately.

"I do. You make me very happy."

Sam moved forward, brushing his lips across hers, pressing soft, fluttering kisses along her jaw as his fingers sifted through her hair. She let out a soft cry of surprise when he stood, taking her with him as he stepped away from the island.

"Making you happy makes me happy," he whispered against her mouth.

Molly wrapped her arms tighter around him, smiling at the thought of making each other very happy for a long time to come.

Sam had just reached the threshold of their bedroom when a knock sounded and Tigger bounded from his bed by the fireplace, running for the door.

"Whoever that is?" Sam said, touching his forehead to Molly's. "They don't make me very happy."

Molly laughed as she slid down his body, her feet touching the ground. "How about I get rid of them?"

One side of his mouth tilted up in an adorable half smile. "I'll wait here."

Still smiling, Molly walked across the tiled floor to the door, calming Tigger by picking him up. He'd filled out so much since she'd found him by the dumpster, but he still only weighed about twenty pounds.

Pulling the door open as she shushed her fierce friend, she was surprised to see Sarah and Chris. Tigger immediately switched from protective to through-the-roof excited. He scrambled in Molly's arms, his tongue doing a mad dance to get closer to their guests.

"Hey, Tigger. Oh my. Calm down before you hurt yourself," Sarah said, lowering as Molly set Tigger on the floor. Wagging his tail like he couldn't contain himself, he licked Sarah's hand and then bounced over to Chris.

"Hey, bud. Too bad everyone isn't always this happy to see me," Chris said with a laugh.

Molly stepped back and gestured for them to come in. "This is a pleasant surprise."

Sarah stood and sent Chris a glance. "Sorry to just show up. Someone is acting a little squirrely." She gestured to Chris with her thumb and walked in, removing her coat. *Guess they're staying for a visit.*

Chris looked oddly sheepish as he came in and removed his jacket. Sam came to the entry and said hello.

"What's going on guys?" He put a hand on Molly's shoulder and pulled her into his side.

"According to Sarah, Chris is being weird," Molly said, tipping her head back to look at Sam.

"I didn't actually say weird, but she's not wrong," Sarah said.

Chris made a growly sound that had Molly smiling. "I'm not being weird. We were out for dinner and I suggested we stop by and say hello to friends. You've been saying we don't do enough couples stuff. This is normal, run of the mill couple behavior."

Sarah smiled and stepped into him, pressing a kiss to his cheek. "Well done, Detective. Next time we should just call first though. They may have been…busy."

Chris waved a hand and walked further into the house, knowing the layout as well as Molly and Sam. "Nah. They live together now. The magic is gone."

Molly started to retort but she saw the way Sarah's smile dimmed, her mouth tightening into a grim line.

Sam followed Chris. "Speak for yourself, man. You may be boring to live with, but our magic is just fine."

"You tell him, babe," Molly said, pulling Sarah by the arm to get her to join them. She leaned in and, using a quieter voice, asked, "You okay?"

Sarah nodded as they walked into the living room. "I am. He just seems…off."

Tigger bounced around the living room, bringing Sarah and Chris his favorite chew toys. Sarah sat down on the carpet in front of the fireplace and played tug of war with him. Chris sat near her, choosing the armchair, smiling warmly at his girlfriend. He did seem to have an unusual energy about him, but there was nothing but genuine affection in his gaze when he looked at Sarah.

Sam pulled Molly down beside him on the couch. "Sit close or they'll think our relationship has gone stale."

Molly laughed and leaned into him. "I don't care what anyone else thinks."

"That's my girl."

"See, Chris," Sarah said, still playing with Tigger. "Not all relationships are doomed once you take the next step."

Chris's mouth dropped open. "I didn't say they were. I don't think that. I was just giving Sam and Molly a hard time."

Molly nodded. "He does like to do that."

"Back at you," Chris said with a smile. He turned to Sarah. "I don't think that. Just to be clear."

Sarah grinned and Molly had to laugh again. They were cute together, and that was an adjective she'd never thought to apply to Chris. Not that he wasn't attractive. He was, but he had an edge and Sarah softened it. Threw him off his game a little, sort of like Sam did with her.

"You guys want to play a game or something? I just bought a new one," Molly said.

"Uh, actually, we probably won't stay long," Chris said. He leaned back in the seat, then leaned forward, rubbing the back of his neck with his hand.

"Are you okay?" Molly leaned forward, looking at him and noticing how…tense he seemed. His jaw was tight, he was fidgety, and he kept darting glances at them—all highly atypical behaviors.

"Yeah. Just…" he said, then stopped. He looked at Sam. "The community raised enough money for Judd's bail."

Sam's body tightened against Molly's. "I saw. I'm glad. I don't care what evidence you found. I can't see it. Hopefully, he'll get a good lawyer."

Chris nodded and locked eyes on Molly. Goosebumps dotted her skin as he held her gaze. "He's had a couple of pro bono offers from what I heard. The evidence against him is fairly incriminating but circumstantial, which is why I think he was let out on bail."

He continued to stare and Molly felt Sam and Sarah fade into the background. Something was going on. Chris shuffled forward in the chair, just a tad.

"Circumstantial. Is that good or bad?" Molly asked.

"Bad if you're the prosecutor. Good if you're the one being charged. But either way, it doesn't stop a man we all respect and admire from possibly going through a murder trial."

It wasn't like Chris to be torn. He was black and white and clearly saw right and wrong in most situations. This must have been eating away at him.

"What evidence?" She held her breath, not sure he'd answer.

"He texted Magnolia, said he needed to see her and that she owed him at least that. They argued over text. He was found at the scene, hovering over her body. He left incriminating evidence at the scene. And apparently they have a history that goes back a few decades."

"A history?" Molly asked.

Chris nodded. "Years ago, Judd lent some money to Magnolia. She never paid up. We'd already found most of the stuff connected to him, but then Magnolia's daughter came into the station with a journal she'd found. Apparently, she liked to keep them, detailing her life and exploits like some sort of tell-all. According to her daughter, and the journals after I saw them, Magnolia was scared of Judd. Said she felt like he was watching her from afar, that he couldn't let bygones be bygones. That was her last entry."

"Seems like a slam dunk," Molly whispered, a chill racing through her.

"It does, doesn't it? All the evidence right there in front of me. Easiest case I've worked in forever."

"That's a good thing, isn't it?" Molly tried to stare harder, to read his mind. What was he getting at?

Chris folded his hands together, letting them hang between his knees. "Of course. That's what we're paid to do. Solve crimes, get criminals off the streets. With the election coming up, it's important we utilize the resources we have in the areas we need. Summer is coming, tourists are on their way. This case is open and shut. It'll take some time for the hearing and sentencing, but as far as the department is concerned, the killer has been found."

"Which means Judd has to live with this hanging over him, and possibly go to jail for something he didn't do," Molly said. *And the department couldn't spend time or money looking for someone else.*

"Okay, you two are being cryptic. What secret messages are you passing?" Sam ran a hand down Molly's hair.

She wasn't entirely sure of the answer, and she didn't want to misstep and make Chris mad. She was working on her longest stretch yet without getting under his skin.

"Nothing," Chris said, too innocently. "I'm just telling you guys this case is open and shut. I want my citizens to feel safe in this town. I can't afford to be wasting my resources or time on this when there are other things to focus on and the prosecution is already sizing Judd for his jumpsuit."

"Off the record, do you really think he did it?" Sam asked, leaning forward, mirroring Chris. "We *know* this man. He helped us out of scrapes and jams, he never hurt a living thing, he's always got a joke on standby and a happy smile."

Chris turned his gaze on Sam. "I have to go with the evidence. Does it seem strange to me that it took no effort at all to figure it out? Does it seem strange that after all these years, new stories about Judd's supposed plan of revenge against Magnolia are coming to light when we've never seen an aggressive side to him? Yes. It does. But what else can I do?"

Molly smiled. "You can't do anything. But someone else could, maybe, dig a little deeper, because from what you're saying, things aren't adding up. Or, they're adding up a little too easily."

Chris smiled, and for the first time since he'd walked in, it seemed genuine. He leaned back in the seat. "Now, Molly. What have I told you about interfering in my cases?"

"To stay out of it."

"And have you ever listened?"

She grinned. "Not well." And if she was reading him right, he didn't want her to this time either.

He shrugged. "Not much I can do about you digging around looking for something to clear Judd. As I said, our resources are limited and I have to focus on what's right in front of me. Not the fact that Magnolia had several enemies. Everyone from her neighbors at the retirement home where she lives to her own children seemed to have a vendetta against her. You can't step sideways without bumping into someone Magnolia rubbed the wrong way."

Sam straightened. "Wait a second. Are you asking Molly to try to find the real killer?" He covered Molly's hand with his own.

Chris looked at his friend. "I would never ask a citizen of my county to do my job. You've heard me, many times in the past, tell Molly that I can do my own job and I don't want her in any danger. I'd never suggest she put herself in a bad situation. But it seems to me, as an editor at a paper that claims to share all sides of the story, that she might have to do a little more digging if she wants that to remain true."

"And what if I find another side to this story?" Molly's skin tingled. Why did she like to solve puzzles and possibly court danger? Well, she could do without the danger, but she couldn't deny the rush it gave her to connect dots and make pieces slide together into a complete image.

"Then you'd bring that information to me as quickly as possible. And it'd have to be pretty convincing. I don't have time for theories and conjecture.

I can't waste my time with hear-say. Even if Debra Connors's alibi didn't quite check out or, according to my sources, her children stand to inherit far more money than anyone realized Magnolia had, there's nothing concrete connecting them to the murder."

Molly glanced at Sam, who looked wary, and Sarah, who just sat there smiling and rubbing Tigger's belly. Chris was asking for her help. And if she wasn't mistaken, he'd just given her a lead to her first three suspects.

Chapter Twelve

Molly picked up a double chocolate shake from Callan's ice cream shop before climbing in her Jeep to head to the retirement center. Until the car show at the end of last summer, Molly had never explored this side of town. This time, though, instead of turning right, which led to the RV and trailer park, Molly went straight. Left would take her to the homeless shelter, an industrial area, and a lot of farmland. She knew the retirement place overlooked the ocean, but she was surprised to see there was also a nine-hole golf course. She wondered if it belonged to the facility or the city.

Either way, it was nice to see, as she walked from her Jeep to the doors, that several seniors were out enjoying the surprisingly sunny day. She was there under the guise of doing more in-depth interviews for the actors in the play, but her real intention included finding out who might have reason to kill Magnolia. She'd decided to start with Deb for two reasons: she was more approachable than Magnolia's children, and she remembered hearing rumors about the two women arguing over a man who also lived on the premises.

The building was a two-story, L-shape with well-kept grounds and a lovely view of the ocean. Even with the sun, this close to the water the breeze swept up around Molly. Inside, the reception area looked more like a hotel than a seniors' residence. High-backed bench seating was arranged in a conversational style, facing each other so people could sit and chat, creating an immediate welcoming feel. Something akin to a reception desk lined the back wall where an insignia of two people embracing caught her eye. It was one of those metal wall art designs, and it struck Molly as quite elegant. She didn't know where the seniors in Britton Bay were getting their money, but she would bet some of Bella's lemon loaf this place came with a huge price tag.

"Hello," a young woman with dark shoulder-length hair greeted. She looked like she'd spent several hours in the sun, and Molly wondered if she'd recently been out of Britton Bay. There hadn't been a lot of tanning weather. "Welcome to The Next Step. Are you visiting someone who resides with us?"

"Hi. Yes, I am. My name is Molly Owens. I'm with the *Britton Bay Bulletin*. I called ahead and mentioned I'd like to interview some of your residents who are participating in the spring play." She pulled her press lanyard out of her purse and showed the woman.

"Ahh, yes. Nice to meet you. I really like the changes you've made to the newspaper. I love the opinion column and your online presence," she said. Her name tag read Yvonne.

"Thank you, Yvonne. I appreciate that. Would it be possible for you to let Debra Connors and Beau Harrison know I'm here?"

"They're already waiting in the dining area," Yvonne said. She pointed down the hallway to Molly's left. "Just head that way. It'll be on the left across from the elevators."

"Thanks so much."

The dining area resembled a cafeteria, but instead of people just eating there were several tables of people playing checkers, chess, and cards. Fortunately, Molly recognized Debra and Beau from the rehearsal she'd seen bits of. They were holding hands and laughing about something, their equally gray heads bent close together.

Weaving around the tables, Molly smiled at those who looked her way and approached the older couple.

"Hi there. I'm Molly Owens with *The Bulletin*," she said.

They pulled apart and looked up at her with easygoing smiles. *No murderous vibes yet.*

Beau stood, offering his seat even though there were two empty ones at the table. "Nice to meet you. Please, have a seat, dear."

Molly sat and Beau took the chair closest to Debra. She reached out and shook each of their hands.

"It's a pleasure to meet you," Debra said. "You look familiar."

"I was helping out with painting the set," Molly said, setting the camera on the tabletop and her bag on the empty chair.

"Before the murder," Debra said, nodding.

Jody Holford

Okay, no skirting around it. "Yes. I'm terribly sorry about Magnolia. I've never been in a play but I've heard that the cast and crew can become very close."

Debra rolled her eyes and made a slight scoffing sound but Beau's lips turned down.

"Terrible thing," he said.

Debra's shoulders stiffened, putting the slightest bit of distance between her and Beau. "Poetic justice."

Molly covered her surprise with a cough. "Excuse me?"

"Deb," Beau admonished, his eyes turning fierce. "It's not right to speak ill of the dead."

"It is when she did all she could while she was alive to make my life miserable," the woman replied.

Molly felt like she was watching a television show, simply observing from behind the screen.

"You just let her get all up in your feathers," Beau said, smoothing a hand down her back. Or…her feathers.

Molly bit her lip to keep from smiling at the image that popped into her brain. "So, you weren't a fan. That much is clear. I guess the police talked to everyone after they realized it was a murder?"

Deb turned her attention back to Molly. "We went back into the station the morning after. Repeated our statements. But Judd —I always knew there was something creepy about Judd—was arrested almost immediately."

From Chris's earlier hint, Molly gathered that whatever statement Deb had given before Judd was arrested was a lie. But why would she have lied if she hadn't known that Magnolia had been murdered before that news went public?

Molly opened her notebook and picked up her pen. "Well, thank goodness it got wrapped up quickly. I'm so glad no one else was on set at the time."

Debra glanced away but it was Beau who spoke. "A blessing. Who knows what would have happened."

Molly looked up again, smiling at him. "Were you guys together? Heading to rehearsal? It was a horrible scene to stumble on, I can tell you that."

Debra's eyes narrowed. Beau pulled her closer, his fingers tightening around the woman's shoulders. "I'm sorry you had to go through that, dear. It's awful. Just awful. Fortunately for us, rehearsal never starts until seven. My Deb was getting her hair cut and colored. I was playing a round of golf when I got the news. Just terrible."

Chris must have checked on her hair alibi and found a hole. "You know," Molly said. "I don't mean to get off topic and I'll get to the interview in just a moment, but I've been putting off getting a haircut. You know how it is when you have to find a new stylist. Who does yours?"

If she hadn't been looking right at Debra, she may have missed the way the woman's eyes widened. She wouldn't, however, have missed the way Beau's head dropped and how he took up a sudden fascination with his fingers on the table.

"Oh, our hair is so different. I don't think you'd do well with my girl. Besides, she does her hair out of her house. She's a good friend of mine. There is a place about twenty minutes from here, a few blocks off of Main Street—Lox. I'd try them. Or if you're desperate, Crazy Cuts."

Molly nodded, wrote down Lox for show. "Okay, thanks. What's your friend's name?"

"Why?" The word was sharp.

Molly put on her most innocent smile. "I just wondered if she was in the play, too."

Debra's features softened. "Oh. Yes, actually. She is." She leaned forward. "Cora. Cora Lester."

Molly wrote down Cora's name before flipping to the interview questions she'd made up. She remembered now that Cora was a hairdresser. She'd heard it more than once in passing. Molly also remembered, quite distinctly, that Cora and Deb were *not* friends.

Moving quickly through both interviews, she noted that Beau and Deb finished each other's sentences with the ease of a long-term couple. If she weren't a little wary of Debra, she'd find them quite sweet.

Standing to leave, she snapped her fingers. "I keep forgetting to ask someone. With Magnolia's passing, who has taken over as director?"

Beau leaned back in his seat, stifling a yawn. "Oh, that sweet girl, Tiffany. She's a born director. Getting her chance to shine, now isn't she? Magnolia had people set to come out all the way from La-La Land to watch the opening night. Reckon Magnolia will still get the credit, what with Tiffany only taking over the week before, but it'll be her that does the meet and greets with the big shots."

Well, Molly thought as she gathered her things, *didn't that just work out perfectly for Tiffany.*

* * * *

Molly returned to *The Bulletin* at the same time as Jill. They walked through the front entrance together, finding Elizabeth and Hannah working together at the layout table.

Hannah smiled and waved. "You're back. How were your interviews?"

Jill hung her bag on the coat hook by her desk. "Mine was good. I went and talked to Judd. He's doing surprisingly well for someone who just got out of jail."

"I'm glad to hear that," Elizabeth said.

"Is he married?" Molly slipped off her coat.

"No. Never has been. He lives over on Fairway in the same house he grew up in," Jill said. She flopped into her leather rolling chair, sending it back a bit.

"I hate to think of him living alone," Molly said. "Especially right now."

"His cousin lives with him," Jill said. "He was there, too. He wants us to run something in the newspaper to thank the community for standing by Judd. He also asked if I knew anything about suing the Sheriff's Department."

Molly leaned against the doorjamb to her office. "Hmm. I suppose if he's wrongfully accused and convicted and that comes to light, he might have a case."

"It'll be a long road. From what I've heard, it's not looking good," Alan said, coming out of his office to join them.

Molly was dying to tell them that even Chris didn't think Judd was the real killer, but she knew how fast word spread in this town. Chris was trusting her to do some digging under the radar. Sharing the information with a room full of people who enjoyed puzzle solving as much as she did was asking for trouble. Most importantly, if word spread, it could alert the killer.

She had more suspects than she'd started the day with, but what she really needed to do was speak to Judd. Her phone buzzed so she slipped into her office, letting the others carry on with their conversation.

Sam: How much do you love me?

Molly grinned as she typed.

Molly: I'm not sure there's an accurate way to measure it. How much do you love me?

Sam: Enough that even if you were one hundred miles away and craving lemon loaf, I'd bring it to you.

Molly's smile widened.

Molly: Are you one hundred miles away craving lemon loaf?

Sam: Not quite. More like fifteen miles and needing an inch and a half wrench that I thought was in my toolbox. In exchange, I will bring you all the lemon loaf you want from here on out.

Her heart swooned even as her stomach reminded her, she needed to eat.

Molly: How about I bring both? Where are you?

Sam: Granger Farm. You take a left instead of the right that takes you to the RV park.

Molly: On my way.

Molly: Also?

Sam: ...Yes?

Molly: I love you more than lemon loaf.

Chapter Thirteen

The Granger Farm was one of several in the area that provided fresh produce to the local businesses. The farm to table initiative sweeping the nation had arrived in Britton Bay long before it was cool and was born mostly out of necessity. The town enjoyed being self-sufficient in as many ways as possible.

Driving under the large sign pitched across two wooden fences, Molly wove her way through one of the driving trails toward the red barn. There were two other paths, one leading to the main house and the other leading to the gardens. Mr. Granger had four barns, all primary colors. Molly smiled at the vibrancy of it all.

Pulling up beside the barn, she waved at a ranch hand she'd seen around town now and again. She didn't see Sam right away even though she was looking at the enormous tractor. She wasn't sure she'd ever seen one that size. Sam came out from around the side as she was getting out of her Jeep. A couple of lab puppies came running over to Molly.

"Oh, hello!" Crouching down, she rubbed them, or tried to. They were so squirmy, it was almost impossible. "You guys are so cute."

"I was thinking the same thing about you," Sam said, wandering over. She glanced up at him, her heart giving its usual fist pump of "yeah-he's-mine." Wearing a plaid shirt over a white t-shirt and torn jeans, he looked like he could be on the cover of a calendar. A car and truck calendar, obviously.

"My ears are not nearly this floppy," Molly said, holding the darker pup's face between her hands. "You are too cute, mister."

"That there is a Miss, and she'd be happy to climb in your pretty little Jeep and head on home with you if you like her that much," a tall, gangly man with a long salt and pepper beard said.

Sam laughed, the sound making Molly smile as she stood up.

"I'm not sure we need another dog underfoot. Or over-foot, if the next is anything like the one we have at home," Sam said, leaning down to play with the pups.

"Oh, come on now," the man she assumed was Mr. Granger said. "One is more work than two. You get more than one and they have a playmate."

Molly grabbed Sam's tool, which she'd swung by his shop to pick up, and brought it over before introducing herself.

"I'm Molly Owens." Her heart was still a little stuck on Sam calling Tigger theirs. They were really building a life together, and though she'd lived with a man before, this felt different. More solid. *Real.*

"Nice to meet you. Heard a lot about you from several people. You'd probably call them sources," he said, laughing as he shook her hand. "John Granger."

Molly passed Sam the tool and went back to loving up the dogs. "I would call them sources actually, unless they were friends. Speaking of which, I heard you were having some trouble with your barns."

Sam stroked a hand affectionately down her hair. "Sorry, John. She can't help herself. The half of her that isn't in story-finding mode is just plain nosy."

Molly laughed and gave Sam's thigh a shove. "Hey."

He looked down at her. "Am I wrong?"

She looked over at John. "He's not."

John looked back at the blue barn and gestured with his thumb. "Figured it out. We have a load of barn cats and it turns out they've been scrapping in the hay. Couple of the mamas are pretty protective since they've had kittens. I think that's what the issue was."

Molly couldn't help the automatic squeeze of her heart. She clasped her hands together. "Kittens?" Her voice went up an octave and Sam laughed, pressing a kiss to the side of her head.

John chuckled. "You're welcome to wander in and take a look. They're cute. You want one, it's yours."

Molly glanced at Sam. "We really don't need a second animal."

"Even if we did, I'm allergic to cats," he said.

The puppies continued to chase each other around and Molly looked their way. *No. No more animals right now.* Sam laughed, probably reading her mind.

She smiled at him and pointed to the barn. "I'll just take a peek."

She wasn't sure how the other barns were utilized, but the blue one seemed to be more storage than anything else. Bales of hay, machines, tools, boxes, and equipment filled the space. Several cats immediately greeted her, weaving around her legs and asking for attention.

She stroked a black and white one who was particularly vocal. "Hey there. Are you a mama cat?" Molly moved slowly through the barn. It was a maze of discarded items, some of the paths barely big enough to stroll through. In one corner behind a large headboard, she found a group of tabbies snuggling up to their mom. The mom looked up with lazy disinterest.

"Oh, aren't you cute?" There were four of them, so small and furry Molly's fingers itched to stroke them. She didn't though, not wanting to upset the mom. A sound behind her—something shifting—startled her into turning around.

A large gray cat had hopped up onto a pile of boxes and was licking his paw. Molly walked toward him and reached out a hand to pet him. He allowed it, making her smile. When he turned and jumped off of the boxes, she watched him go, wondering if maybe there was another litter of kittens nearby. Molly followed after the cat, winding her way into one of the corners of the barn. In the back of her mind, she wondered if all of this stuff shoved into the outbuilding could be a potential fire hazard.

Another cat jumped up onto a sawhorse. Long sheets of plywood were leaned against it. Leaning over to pet him, she caught a glimpse of hay and blankets behind the wood, shoved into a corner, with a torn and tattered item of clothing—maybe a jacket—bunched up like a make-shift pillow. She tried to move closer but the only way to do so would have been to slip under the sawhorse and move the plywood to the side. Glancing around, Molly saw only cats. Maybe the dogs goofed around in this barn. Tigger loved to drag a blanket into a corner and muss it around.

"Molly?" Sam called.

Turning, she saw him in the doorway, the sun at his back. "You okay?"

She nodded, making her way over to him. "Yes. Just checking out all the kitty hiding spots. Does John have kids?" This barn, despite the multitude of less-than-safe items, would make a perfect spot for hide-and-seek or a game of make-believe.

When she reached Sam, he put both hands to her hips and pulled her a little closer, but not so she was touching him. He didn't look like he'd gotten grease on his clothes, but she appreciated his caution.

"He does. They're older though. Seventeen and fourteen. I'm just about finished here. You want to grab something to eat?"

That was a little old for make-believe and make-shift beds in the corner of a cluttered garage.

"Babe?" He kissed the tip of her nose.

Molly blinked. "Why don't I bring something home and we'll take Tigger for a walk. Maybe eat on the beach?"

"Sounds perfect. I'll meet you at home. I'm going to swing by and pick up the cake from Bella first."

He walked her to her Jeep, and after a heartfelt, roll-over-their-own-paws goodbye with the pups, Molly headed for Calli's to grab take-out.

* * * *

"Talk to me," Sam said in between a bite of his pastrami sandwich.

They'd spread a large blanket out on the sand. With the waves cresting in front of them and the sun setting over the water, it was both peaceful and romantic. Tigger gnawed on a piece of driftwood as close to the blanket as he could get without getting in trouble for being on it. Wet dog, sand, and food did not mix well. Every now and again, he'd glance at them longingly, and when he thought Molly wasn't looking, Sam would send a chip his way.

"What would you like to talk about?" Molly smiled at him, picking up her lemonade for a long, quenching drink.

Sam tilted his head. He was so handsome with his dark hair always in need of a bit of a trim, his dark brown eyes, and square jaw. Just a hint of stubble graced it today. She liked him that way. Or any way at all. He'd changed into a University of Portland sweater Jill had given him when she'd come home for good. A few teens were playing Frisbee further down the beach, closer to the pier, their shouts and laughter mingling with the waves.

"Are we going to pretend you're not digging into something dangerous?" He picked up another chip.

Sam was fairly understanding of Molly's more curious side. That didn't mean he enjoyed the close calls she'd had. Not that she did. But this was more personal for him. Not only was his girlfriend digging into a supposedly solved case, but it was for a man he admired. She remembered how it had turned out with the last man Sam admired. The co-founder of the car show Sam had hosted last summer had wound up dead. Shortly before, they'd met with him and found out he wasn't the most upstanding of human beings. She'd hated the disappointment Sam had felt. She hoped Judd wouldn't be another example of someone her boyfriend admired not being who they seemed.

"Come on, Molly. On top of worrying about you, I want Judd cleared."

"It's eerie how you do that," Molly said.

"What?"

"Read my mind. I was just thinking about both of those things. You worrying about me and thinking about Judd. I want you to know, I don't plan on putting myself in danger. I've had enough of that to last a lifetime."

Sam brushed his fingers off on his jeans and reached up to cup Molly's cheek. "It seems to find you, regardless. But I'm glad you have no intention of searching for it. I've grown pretty fond of you."

Molly leaned into his palm. "Back at you. Are you mad Chris asked me?"

Sam sighed, bent his knees, and rested his forearms on them, staring out at the ocean. "I understand why he did. You're good at figuring things out. People talk to you. And I truly don't think he'd throw you into the lion's den. Even if he was mad at you." He looked at her, a cute smirk lifting his lips. "But if he's right, if it wasn't Judd, trying to find out *who* will put you in danger no matter what. I'd like to know what you know. Not just for Judd but because I'd rather you didn't do anything on your own in regard to this."

It was in her nature to bristle. She'd been roaming around on her own for longer than she could remember. But she wasn't on her own anymore, and she had to remind herself that if the situation were reversed, she'd want to have Sam's back. He wasn't asking her to stop or change part of herself. He was asking not to be cut out.

Glancing around, Molly scooted closer. "Deb Connors was definitely lying about her alibi. Her boyfriend, Beau Harrison was hiding something as well. I can't figure out if they're covering for each other or they're keeping secrets from each other. Deb thinks Magnolia was after Beau. I've heard that from more than one person. But her alibi is Cora and there's no love lost between them. I haven't spoken to Cora yet, but if she's covering for Deb, there's got to be a reason. Tiffany—the assistant—is now the director, and while that doesn't seem like much of a coup, Magnolia had invited some of her Hollywood connections to the opening."

Sam leaned back on his elbows, still looking at Molly. "That's three possible suspects."

Brushing her hands off, she started packing up the remnants of their picnic. "Plus, the son and daughter. I'm going to go out to Magnolia's mansion tomorrow to talk with Jeffrey and Vivien. I've told them I have some follow-up questions for the story on their mom."

"Five other suspects and Judd is the front runner?"

Molly nodded. "Right? All of these other suspects and all evidence conveniently points to a man who, other than a few texts, she had nothing to do with for years. Even if he was angry about the money from years ago, why kill her over it? How much could it have been? I need to talk to Judd."

"I'll go with you," Sam said, sitting up.

"Okay. Might be easier if you contacted him and set that up. He's only met me in passing."

"I can do that," Sam said, his eyes still looking a little distant.

Molly took his hand and brought it to her lips. "Look at us, solving mysteries together."

Sam laughed and removed his hand, putting it around her shoulder and pulling her close. "Never a dull moment with you. What do you suppose normal couples do for fun?"

She tilted her head back, resting it on his arm so she could look at him. "You saying I'm not normal?"

He leaned in, kissed her. "You're unique and normal is boring."

"Nice save," she said, kissing him back.

Tigger barked for attention. When Molly glanced over at him, his butt was up in the air, wiggling, the front of his body hunched, as he watched them, wanting in on the affection.

"Come here, then," Molly said. The food was away and she couldn't say no to those eyes.

Tigger bounced over to them, crawling right up in Molly's lap and putting his front paws on Sam's arm, trying to sniff his face. Sam laughed and rubbed the dog's head.

"No more for you, mister."

"You think he needs a friend?" Molly asked.

Sam's eyes locked on hers over Tigger's head. "It wouldn't suck. Having two instead of one. Would you want that?"

She shrugged. "Our place is kind of small. Tigger's a good size but I'm not sure having a lab is a good idea. They get big. And I'm not sure your mom would be thrilled about that."

Watching, and reading, Sam's face, she noted that he was choosing his words carefully. "My mom could be persuaded, I'm sure. But I agree, a lab might be too big. You don't want to look for another place, do you?"

"Not really. I love it here." She shook her head. "Never mind. I'm just being silly. We don't need more complications." She rubbed Tigger vigorously then leaned over to grab his driftwood and toss it down the beach for him.

As her adorable dog ran off, Sam turned and pulled her onto his lap. "I want to complicate my life as much as possible with you."

Molly laughed. "Is that a compliment?"

Sam leaned in and pressed his forehead to Molly's. She liked the connection and took a second to breathe him in while he found his words.

"It is. Even if it didn't come out that way. I love living with you. You want another dog; we'll make it work. You want five more dogs; we'll probably have to consider a bigger place but we'd make it work. Whatever you want, Molly."

Putting both of her hands to his face, she gazed into his eyes, her heart flipping over with a giant thud. "What do you want?"

Sam kissed her, one hand curling around the nape of her neck. "You. That's all I've wanted since the moment I watched you get out of your Jeep. It overwhelms me sometimes, how much I love you."

Her heart practically vibrated with happiness. "I feel the same. It scares me."

"I know. But it should scare you less that it's mutual, right?"

She laughed softly, kissing one cheek, then the other. "You'd think."

"We can think about the dog. I'll talk to my mom. But I think you're right that if we do, we should go smaller."

The little nomadic piece of herself that still rumbled around occasionally wasn't panicking over the idea of such a big step. *You live with him. How could getting an animal be a big step?* It was another level of commitment. Picking out a dog together, bringing one home, with the assumption they'd be together for its whole long life.

"There it is," Sam said, laughing softly as Tigger flopped down beside them.

"What?"

He pressed his index finger to the wrinkle between her brows. "The worry line that shows up whenever you think too hard about the future."

Her heart snagged. "Don't ever doubt that I want one with you."

He sighed. "I don't. I truly don't. One step at a time. We've moved pretty quick so far. We've got time for the rest of it."

Urgency chugged through her veins. "Whatever the rest of it is? I want it with you. I love you, Sam."

"I love you back, Molly."

And he did. So much. The last relationship she'd had didn't feel anything like this one, even at the height of being good. It had ended badly and she'd done what she always did, picked up and left. But if something went sideways with Sam, would she be able to do that? Because the truth was, she was tied not only to him but to the town. Could they co-exist if something went badly? Could she watch him walk down the street with someone else at his side?

"Stop it, Molly," he whispered.

She loved and hated that he read her so well. "I don't want to mess this up."

"Then we won't."

She believed him. That was the biggest difference between Sam and any other man she'd been with. Tigger lightened the mood by trying to hoover up whatever crumbs they'd left on the blanket.

In the back of Molly's brain, her thoughts zigzagged, stuck on the idea of what if. What if Judd was madly in love with Magnolia years ago and she had brushed him off then and now? Molly didn't want to imagine a life where she and Sam weren't each other's, but would either of them feel resentment? Hatred? No. Most people wouldn't. Most people would move on. Unless the person that ripped your heart out came back one day, only to do it again. Was that enough to make a person snap? *Not helpful thoughts toward someone you're trying to clear.* She needed to talk to Judd. She needed to hear what he felt toward Magnolia from his own lips. She needed to look into his eyes as he told her he didn't do it. And then she needed to help Chris find a way to prove it. If she believed him.

Chapter Fourteen

The mansion was worthy of a Hollywood legend. Since learning about the play, Molly had read all she could about Magnolia Sweet online. She'd been confused at first by the woman's attitude in relation to the number of acting credits she held. After starring in some commercials at the age of eighteen, she'd landed a five-year spot on a well-loved soap opera. She'd been fired for a variety of things—all conjecture from the tabloids. But after that, her career had been sporadic at best. So how, Molly wondered, had she pulled off acting like such a diva when she'd settled back in a small town in the middle of practically nowhere?

Molly rang the bell again, staring at the frosted glass doors that were double her height at least. The answer, she'd found, was in producing. Magnolia had still maintained a wide reach, despite living on the Oregon coast. No one truly knew why she'd left Hollywood, but she had invested wisely and helped produce several box office hits over the last ten years.

The door swung open and a man in tennis shorts and runners answered. Molly's eyes widened, mostly in surprise at seeing a half-naked, impressively chiseled chest when she'd been expecting Vivien. His aggrieved expression morphed immediately into a charming smile.

"You don't look like any girl scout I've ever seen," he said, his voice low. Was it a failed attempt at sounding seductive?

Molly had her lanyard in the inside pocket of her purse. She flashed it and returned his smile with a much more sedate one of her own. "Molly Owens from the *Britton Bay Bulletin*. I believe you and your sister were expecting me?"

"Oh. Right. The reporter. What's one more? Come on in. I'm Jeffrey." He held the door and stepped back, ushering Molly in with much less enthusiasm.

"I'm actually the editor of the paper, but I spoke with your sister when she came to see me about your mom. I'm so sorry for your loss," Molly said.

Jeffrey shut the door and stared at Molly a beat too long. Her skin prickled uncomfortably. If she'd had one piece of advice for her younger self, it would be to never ignore that gut reaction. She could have saved herself a lot of trouble if she hadn't. *But you wouldn't be where you are today.*

"Yes, a great loss for all. Did you know my mother?"

"No."

"Me neither."

Molly bit her lip hard to keep from gasping at the blunt and harsh words.

She turned to look at her surroundings, choosing not to reply. White marble tiles gleamed in every direction. A spiral staircase led to a second story, and when she looked up, she saw the opulent chandelier, sparkling like glistening raindrops.

"Your home is beautiful," she said. To the right was a sunken seating area. The furnishing was large. All of it. The oversized couches looked like they'd never been sat in. A sculpture of a life-size giraffe seemed out of place near the window. Interesting. Eclectic. Odd.

"It'll be on the market by the end of next week if you're interested," Jeffrey said.

Molly smiled. "Bit out of my price range. Are you sorry to see it go?"

Jeffrey walked to the banister and picked up the gray T-shirt lying over it, holding it between his hands. "We didn't grow up here. My mother had a fondness for this town, and when she needed to leave L.A., she purchased this place. We didn't spend much time here."

She couldn't tell if his monotone voice was hiding emotion or showing he held none. The click-clack of heels pulled Molly's attention to the large arched opening to her left.

Vivien smiled as she approached. "Molly, right?" When she reached out to shake hands, hers was much less glamorous than the last time Molly had seen her. No crimson nails.

"Yes. Nice to see you again." Molly dropped her hand.

She sent a glance toward her brother and frowned. "Put your shirt on. We have company."

Jeffrey scowled but did what she said.

When she noticed Molly looking at her hands, Vivien wiggled the fingers of one. "Packing is hell on the hands."

"I can't believe how much stuff she has," Jeffrey said from behind them.

Vivien turned to Jeffrey like she was irritated with him just for being there, wrinkling her nose. "I thought you'd have showered after your workout."

He shrugged. "What's the point? I'm just going to get sweaty again lugging boxes. Don't know about you ladies, but I could use a drink."

Vivien gestured for Molly to follow Jeffrey.

"We'll use the sunroom, Jeffrey."

He mumbled something Molly figured was agreement. They certainly had an interesting dynamic. The rest of what she saw of the house was every bit as luxurious as the foyer and sitting room. The kitchen looked like something off of the Food Network with its long, wide counters, double ovens, and catering-size fridge.

"This is amazing. Did your mom like to cook?"

Jeffrey opened the fridge and pulled out a pitcher of what looked like iced tea. "No. But she liked to entertain, and no matter what, people always end up in the kitchen somehow, right?"

Molly nodded. That was actually quite true of any get-togethers she could recall. While Jeffrey poured all of them a drink, Molly pulled her notepad from her bag. "I appreciate you guys taking the time to let me follow up on a couple of things. I know you have so much going on and it's such a hard time for you."

Jeffrey passed the two women tea and gulped his down, pouring a second. "It's an inconvenience for sure. Viv and I have a lot on our plate right now."

Molly took a sip of her tea to hide her reaction. *Ah, yes. Death, the great inconvenience to one's schedule.*

"Nothing we can't handle. It's nicer in the sunroom, but we have appointments this afternoon, so we'll need to make this meeting quick," Vivien said. Like her mother, she clearly had no issues being in charge.

"Of course." Molly trailed after them, through the kitchen to a set of French doors that led out to a glass-enclosed patio. An in-ground pool at one end rivaled the size of Molly's home. Jeffrey waited for the women to sit on the outdoor sofa before sitting across from them in a matching chair.

Molly set her drink down and got started. "I was thinking about adding a bit more of a personal element to your mother's dedication page. There's so much about her work, but I wondered if you had any anecdotes you'd like to add. Perhaps a funny conversation or memory? An auto-correct mishap that makes you smile when you remember it? I just thought it might be nice for the people of Britton Bay to see who she was outside of an actress and producer."

Vivien took a deep breath and exhaled it slowly. Jeffrey, who'd set his drink down on a table beside him, gripped the arms of his chair.

"Most of our phone conversations were straight to the point. We work for her, you understand?" Vivien crossed one leg over her knee.

"I didn't know that. You work for her production company? In Los Angeles?"

Vivien nodded. "We do. There was a bit of an...incident, so Mom thought it better to return to Britton Bay. Her wealth goes a lot further in a town like this than L.A. Most of our conversations were work-related and to the point. She couldn't stand texting or emailing. She had an assistant that took care of all email correspondence."

Molly frowned. "Were you aware of a relationship between her and Judd Brown?"

Jeffrey scoffed and picked up his drink. "The killer? There was no relationship. The man is a liar as well as a murderer."

Shifting in her seat, Molly thought of how to phrase the question without getting herself tossed out. "Be that as it may, the police said there were text messages back and forth. How can you be so sure your mom wasn't seeing Judd?"

"Because my mother hated cheaters. Loathed them," Vivien said.

"Judd isn't married," Molly said gently.

"Maybe not. But my mother is," Jeffrey said, then set his drink down. "Was."

Molly's pulse sped up. "She was married? At the time of her death?"

Vivien nodded. "Yes. They were estranged, but that didn't matter. Married is married. We believe mom moved back to Britton Bay to be closer to him."

"Her husband lives here?"

They both nodded. "Yes. He's in the play. Beau Harrison. He's our step-father."

Chapter Fifteen

By the time Sam picked Molly up at *The Bulletin* so they could head over to Judd's house, her mind felt like an overstuffed suitcase. The party prep for the next night was all finished, so that was one thing off their plate. Molly couldn't believe that they'd celebrate a birthday this Saturday and be at a funeral the next.

Leaning over in the cab of Sam's truck, she pressed her lips to his. He hooked his hand behind her neck and pulled her in, taking the kiss deep enough to scramble her thoughts.

"Hi," he said, pulling away and putting the truck in drive.

"Hi. I think that was the best part of my day," she said, settling into her seat.

Sam chuckled and reached over the console to rest his hand on hers on her thigh. "It couldn't have been a very good day then. I wasn't even trying."

Molly laughed and looked over at him. "I won't add to your ego by telling you you're often the best part of my day."

His hand squeezed hers. "You good?"

"I am. How was your day?"

He drove away from town, heading into an older area where the houses didn't look like heritage homes because they'd been renovated. As they wound up the incline of what the locals called the bluffs, the yards got bigger and the buildings got smaller.

"It was good. My mom had Brandon over for lunch today," Sam said with only a slight tightness in his tone.

Brandon Saron was the sheriff of Britton Bay who was currently acting as mayor. When the last mayor had left town, he'd stepped up to take over the position temporarily. He was well suited to the role and well respected in town. Molly liked him, even though she'd been served with more than one warning about poking her curious nose into the wrong places while he'd been sheriff. Sam was struggling with the idea of his mom dating. That she was dating someone he respected made it more difficult to raise concerns.

"He's been great about helping with the party. We should have them for dinner at our place some time. Just the four of us. Speaking of which, I think we should move the desk and get a small table so we actually have a place to eat dinner."

The sun had already begun to set and this area of town wasn't as well lit as Main Street. Many of the houses didn't have exterior lights on, which made it seem even darker. More eerie.

"I like that idea. We can shop for our first piece of furniture together."

Molly turned her hand over and linked her fingers with his. "I love that you actually sound excited about the idea. I've never met a man who liked to shop."

"Easy. I didn't say I liked to shop. But everything about building a life with you excites me, Molly."

It took Molly a moment to recover her breath. "If I wasn't already crazy about you, that would have tipped me over."

He brought her fingers to his lips and kissed them before they settled into the ride. It didn't take long. Britton Bay wasn't huge. The population was somewhere around eighty thousand people, and it was only a twenty-minute ride from one end to the other.

The house they pulled up in front of was well cared for despite its obvious age. A small front porch gave it a welcoming feel even with the slightly slanted set of steps leading up to it.

Sam turned the truck off. "He's probably feeling overwhelmed, so let's tread lightly."

Molly grabbed her bag and looked over at him when the interior light went on. "I'll try to remember to keep my brass knuckles in the bag." She reached out and rubbed Sam's shoulder. "I know he matters to you."

Sam nodded and they got out of the truck and walked up the cemented path. The porch creaked when they stepped onto it. Judd answered the door on the first knock, like he'd been waiting.

"Sam. And it's Molly, right? Come on in."

When Judd closed the door behind them, they stood in the small entryway a moment, shaking hands, Molly and Sam giving awkward condolences. What did one say to someone who'd been accused of murder and was possibly innocent?

"Come on in. Sorry, it's a mess. Can I get you two something to drink? I've got some soda and juice." Judd cleared a bunch of newspaper off of the couch, folded the pages together, and set them in a basket to the side. "Sit."

"I'm fine, thank you," Molly said. She sank farther into the cushions than she expected to and adjusted her position so she could take notes on her pad. Sam sank down beside her and she had to brace her legs so she didn't roll into him.

He smiled at her. "I'm good, too, Judd. We don't need anything. Molly just wants to ask you some questions to see if we can help."

A wide wooden mantle over an aged stone fireplace held framed photographs, but Molly couldn't see who was in them. Books littered the side tables, a reasonable-sized television was angled in the corner, and an arched doorway led to another room she suspected was a kitchen. The slight scent of something burnt lingered in the air.

Judd sat in the overstuffed armchair across from them, brushing his graying hair out of his eyes. "Don't know what help you can give, to be honest. But I appreciate it all the same. Never thought I'd think these four walls would seem like a palace, but let me tell you, in comparison to a six-by-four-foot cell, they're the Taj Mahal."

Molly felt a pang of sorrow but reminded herself to be objective. This man mattered to Sam and Chris, and Chris was an excellent cop who thought there was more to the story. But they could have been wearing blinders that often came with affection.

"I'm sure it's not pleasant. I just wanted to follow up on a couple things. If I ask anything that upsets you, I apologize in advance. My only intention is to try to find the real killer."

Judd looked down at the carpet a moment and Molly sensed he was gathering himself. When he lifted his head, his eyes were watery. "Wouldn't hurt nothing. I know you don't know me but it's the truth. I didn't care for Magnolia. Maybe I did once upon a time but there was never nothing between us."

"We know you didn't hurt anyone, Judd," Sam said.

We hope. "I heard Magnolia was on set every day at four even though rehearsal wasn't until seven. Were you there at that time?"

Judd nodded, clasping his hands between his knees. "Yup. Every day. She was nothing if not particular about her schedule. But I didn't spend any time with her. I kept my distance right from the start. Not that she remembered me, really. That day, I was meeting my cousin Tripp. He was applying for the temp job on the cleaning staff. I was waiting for him at the reception and heard something, so I went in and, well, you know what I found, Molly. I can't get that out of my head."

Judd shifted in his chair and Molly felt another pang of sadness for him. She'd had the image in her head more than a few times too. It wasn't pleasant, and knowing that it had been intentional made it worse.

"I understand that completely. It's awful," Molly said.

Sam reached out and squeezed her hand. "What do you think you heard?"

Judd shrugged. "I reckon the house coming down."

"Did Tripp show up?" Molly asked, making notes.

Judd nodded. "Yeah. The manager rescheduled though, on account of all the police swarming the place."

"So, you *didn't* have a relationship with Magnolia?"

Judd's face scrunched up but he said nothing. Molly watched his hand clench and unclench. The front door opened and closed. All three of them looked toward the entryway and Molly saw a man not much taller than herself shuffle in. He was wearing jeans and a plaid work shirt. His gray hair was receding in a perfect m-shaped arch.

"Oh. Sorry, Jay. Didn't know you had company." The man set a steel lunchbox down and came all the way into the room. "Hey there. You're Sam Alderich, right? Tripp Simmons. I sure loved that car show you put on. Great stuff. Other than the murder, obviously."

"I am, and thanks." Sam shook his hand.

Molly nearly laughed. Tripp cringed at his own words. "Sorry. No disrespect meant."

"I'm Molly." She shook his hand, noting the firm grip.

"How was work?" Judd asked his cousin.

"Lots of gossip. We can talk later. I'll grab a shower and dinner and come back up." Tripp started to back away.

"Actually, Molly here is somewhat of a sleuth and is looking for other suspects. Why don't you stay?" Judd said.

Tripp ran his hand through his bushy hair. "You don't say. How about that. Did you tell her about your locker?"

Molly and Sam both looked toward Judd expectantly.

"What about your locker?"

Judd sat straighter. "Those texts they found between me and Magnolia? I didn't send them or respond to anything she sent me. Most of the time, I couldn't even remember to grab my phone. But even if there was evidence, they can't honestly believe anything was going on. I mean, really, look at me. I'm a janitor, living in the same house I grew up in. Even if I was pining for Magnolia, which I absolutely was not, why would a woman like that be texting with me?"

He had a point. Plus, Molly remembered, the Sweet children had both mentioned their mother's dislike of texting.

"She wasn't a better person than you just because she lived in a fancy house and had money, Judd," Sam said, his voice rigid.

"Amen, brother," Tripp said, taking a seat on the ottoman. "I got a temp job at the rec center just in time. With Judd being on leave, I've been covering his hours. His locker was broken into a while back. He never fixed it. Too busy fixing everything else. But that means someone else could have gotten to his phone, right?"

Molly jotted that down, then looked at Judd. "Most people carry their phones with them."

Judd smiled, his teeth showing through his massive beard. "Most *young* people, dear. I go to work, do my job. I'm not there to chat on the phone or play solitaire, which is really all I use my phone for. Always leave it in my locker. Keep my wallet on me, but there's not much in it, so it's not bulky. Plus, I like to grab some snacks from the vending machine without having to run back to my locker. No reason to have my phone on me. Sometimes I don't even remember to turn it on."

"Were any other prints found on it?" Molly asked.

"They didn't say so," Judd replied.

"Ridiculous. My cousin has been part of this community his whole life. Detective Beatty knows he didn't do this, but he still had to spend a night in a cell."

"Now, Tripp. You calm down. Chris is just doing his job." Judd settled further back into his seat, his tone soft.

Tripp leaned forward on the ottoman. "I've been listening to conversations around the stage, trying to find some proof that someone else did this— guess I'm sort of an amateur sleuth like you, Molly. A lot of people had a grudge against that woman. Haven't heard one person say they were sorry to see her go. Seems like the new director isn't much softer though. I heard she came out from Los Angeles thinking she'd get to shine, and Magnolia did nothing but shove her into the background. Seems like motive to me."

"Tiffany's a nice girl, Tripp. She's hardly had an easy go of it, waiting hand and foot on Magnolia."

Judd seemed to have a soft spot for everyone. He looked at Molly. "Told you I might not be able to help you or myself. I just can't think of anyone who would do this."

"What do you know about Beau Harrison and Debra Connors? Do those names sound familiar?"

Judd smiled but Molly was distracted by Tripp's derisive snort. Judd glanced at his cousin but looked back at Molly. "This is a small town, dear. I grew up with Deb. She was a few years ahead of me. I know Beau from a few senior events I've attended."

Molly made a quick note and smiled at Judd. "I saw there's another senior golf tournament coming up at the course beside their facility."

Judd laughed. "Probably. But that's not my game. Or Beau's, actually. Both of us joined a tournament a few years ago and we were so bad at it we hit the nineteenth hole about three hours early. We decided right then and there we'd never be stepping foot on the greens again. Better ways to use our time."

Molly laughed, knowing that referred to the bar, but then remembered Beau's alibi.

"Were you friends?" Molly asked.

Judd waved a hand. "Friendly, maybe. We didn't really run in the same circles. Why you asking about them? Deb's all bark."

Tripp let out a frustrated huff. "She the one playing Auntie Em? I heard her yelling at Beau today on set. You ask me, she's all bi—"

"Tripp," Judd cut in. "Lady present."

Tripp frowned. "Sorry. Just don't like any of them. Any one of them had reason to kill Magnolia, being bossed around by her all day, but no, they've pinned it on my cousin."

"I'm sure this is hard on both of you. Do you have any other family in the area?" Molly closed her notebook.

"Couple more cousins," Judd said.

"Anyone see you at the time of death?"

Judd shook his head. "Nope. No one was at the front desk when I was waiting for Tripp. When I heard the thud, I went in. No one else was in the theater until you showed up."

"I've got some leads I'm going to follow, Judd. I know that this needs to happen quickly. Sam cares a great deal for you and I want to help any way I can. If you can think of anything else that seems odd or out of place, let me know, okay? You can reach me at the newspaper."

"You're a nice girl, Molly. Sam's a lucky man. Deservedly so." Judd stood and shook both of their hands.

As they were moving toward the exit, Tripp walked next to Molly. "He didn't do this. He wouldn't hurt a fly. My money is on that Deb woman. Nasty to everyone she talks to. No better than Magnolia, you ask me."

Molly stopped and looked at Tripp. "Did you know Magnolia?"

His eyes widened but he shook his head. "Nah. But you don't have to know someone to hear all the stories. Doesn't sound like I was missing out."

Maybe not. She certainly didn't have a whole lot of people in her corner. If any.

"You'll dig into Deb? Maybe that director girl?" Tripp asked.

"I will. I'm glad he has you looking out for him," Molly said.

"Family stands by you no matter what. What's that saying? Blood is thicker than water. He's my blood."

Molly fought the slight cringe the words conjured and nodded her head. Not everyone felt that way. Certainly not Magnolia's own children.

Chapter Sixteen

"We need pie," Molly said as Sam drove back toward Main Street.

He laughed. "It's almost nine o'clock."

Molly glanced at the dash and saw he was right. "Yeah, but Come N' Get It is open until ten, and they serve pie. This proves that after nine isn't an unreasonable time for such a thing. In fact, I'm pretty sure there's no bad time to have pie."

Taking a right at the four way stop, she saw him shake his head in the dark cab. "You do make several good points."

"I knew you'd see it my way."

Molly stared through the windshield at the moon and the passing streetlights, thinking about the different things she'd learned over the last day and a bit. She needed to write everything down or it would swirl around in her brain and drive her nuts. She loved technology and had the same addiction to her phone as everyone else, but when she was sorting through a puzzle or story, she needed to see it on paper.

"I think I can actually hear the gears turning in your brain. What'd you think about Judd?" Sam turned onto Main Street.

"I get why you care for him. It's easy to see. I still think that even people we can't imagine snapping have the ability to do so. We saw that with the car show. And the wedding. And Vernon. Wow. We've seen it a lot."

Sam reached over and took her hand. "We have. And I know you're right. Good people can do really bad things. Judd's not like that though, babe."

She wanted him to be right. She linked her fingers to his, liking the connection. "What struck me was his lack of anger."

"He's not an angry guy," Sam agreed.

"That's just it. If someone is framing him for murder, you'd think he'd be pointing fingers and raging. But he isn't. In fact, he spoke kindly toward almost everyone. That doesn't scream killer to me. Even if Magnolia pushed all of his buttons."

"I'm glad you see that."

Molly swallowed around the lump in her throat. "But he could still be guilty, Sam. We need to be prepared for that."

"I am," he insisted.

As they got out of the truck and walked toward the restaurant, she wondered if any of them could ever be ready for the deep, dark secrets some people kept.

Calli and Dean were sitting in a booth with Sarah and Chris. Molly grinned and looked up at Sam as the door shut behind them.

"See? Never too late for pie."

"You can't see what they're eating." Sam pressed a kiss to her head, laughing at her in a good way. She liked making him smile. Plus, she knew she was right.

As they approached the table, everyone said hello. Obviously having heard them, Sarah held up her plate with a mostly eaten piece of strawberry-rhubarb custard pie.

"Never too late," Sarah said.

Calli and Dean shuffled out of their side of the booth, taking their near-empty sodas with them.

"Sit. We need to clean up anyway. You want some pie, doll?" Calli gave Molly a side hug as she asked.

"Lemon, I think," Molly said, hugging her back.

"I'll have a slice of blueberry peach, if you have it," Sam said.

Molly started to sit but stopped. "Hmm. Maybe I want that one."

Sam rolled his eyes and gave her a little nudge so she slid into the booth. "We can share."

Dean laughed and walked back to the kitchen. Calli smiled at the group. "You want anything else? Chris? You want another coffee, hon?"

"I'm good, Calli. Thanks. Any more and I won't sleep tonight."

"And that would be different from most nights, how?" Sarah asked, scooping up another bite of pie.

Chris put his arm around her shoulder and pressed a kiss to her temple. "Maybe I should switch to warm milk."

Sam's bark of laughter made Molly smile. He slid into the booth. "If you go that way, you might need to start going to bed at seven. Eating dinner at four like the retirees."

Chris crumpled a straw wrapper and tossed it at Sam. Calli shook her head, muttering about boys.

"This is a nice surprise," Molly said, shrugging out of her jacket and stuffing it beside her with her purse.

"Gotta grab the dates where we can. Someone is working overtime all the time," Sarah said. She leaned her head into the crook of Chris's arm.

"That's about to get better."

Sarah sat up and looked at him. Molly and Sam both leaned forward.

Chris shook his head and sighed. "Shouldn't have said that out loud, but you guys will find out at the town hall meeting. Brandon—Sheriff Saron—isn't running for mayor. That means he'll be back where he should be and I'll go back to being a detective."

Sarah smiled and scooted up to kiss his cheek. "That's good. That's really good. You're not disappointed, are you?"

"No. I barely got a chance to put on my detective badge before everything blew up and Brandon had to step up as mayor. I'm happy to work my way up the ranks a little slower," Chris said, picking up his coffee and tipping it back.

Calli brought their pie over. "Should have asked if you two wanted a drink."

Molly smiled, noting that Calli had cut both pieces of pie in half so she and Sam each had a sample. "I'll just have a water. Thank you."

"I'll take the same. Thanks, Calli."

"No problem. When are you two christening that back patio with a BBQ?"

"Good question," Chris said, scooping a piece of Sarah's pie.

"Soon. But you can at least see it tomorrow at the party."

"Between the party and everything else going on, we'll need a nice quiet night with friends on your back deck. When things calm down. No pressure," she said.

After she left them and Molly had taken her first bite of delicious lemon pie, Chris leaned in. "So?"

Molly chewed and swallowed, pausing when Calli dropped off their waters. Dean was on the floor but he was mopping under tables so Molly just focused on their group of four.

"Beau and Deb both lied about their alibis. Beau I'm sure of, and Deb I'm going to confirm tomorrow if I can get Cora to talk to me. I have Jill working on that right now. Magnolia's son seems too...spoiled to have done anything like this himself. His sister makes the decisions, from what I can see. Judd's cousin had a bad feeling about Tiffany and Deb. And I found out some interesting information about Beau." She paused, looking at him and knowing how good he was at his job. "Have you done any digging on Tiffany or Beau?"

Chris smiled and looked like he was scrolling through his thoughts. "Tiffany Faye is twenty-nine, divorced, has worked in film and television, and was born in Utah. She was hired by Magnolia's company to come out here as an assistant for the play. Beau Harrison was born in Portland. Lived in Los Angeles for three years, worked as a grip on the set of Magnolia Sweet's television show. They married fifteen years ago but separated after three years."

Molly's jaw dropped open. Sarah set her fork down with a clang, saying, "Wow. That is a lot of facts and holy drama, Batman."

Chris smirked. "There tends to be a lot of drama around murders, babe."

"Yeah but there's drama and then there's *drama*," Sarah said, drawing the word out the second time she said it.

Sam turned his head, his fork stopped in mid-air. "Did you know Beau and Magnolia were married?"

"Found out today," Molly said.

"Though I don't want to boost your ego in this area because normally I wouldn't condone you digging into things, you're very good at getting people to open up to you, Molly."

She grinned at Chris and straightened in her seat. "Well, thank you, Detective Beatty. You're pretty good at this stuff, too."

Sam laughed, taking his bite of pie. Sarah laughed, covering her mouth with her hand and Chris just gave an exasperated sigh and shook his head. Molly caught a hint of a smile on his lips though.

"Any chance you can find out if Beau stands to inherit anything from Magnolia's death?"

Chris nodded. "I'll ask around tomorrow."

"In other news," Sarah said, "not to drag us away from murder and intrigue, but how are things going with your mom and Brandon, Sam? I ran into him shopping for a card for her and he looked more than a little smitten."

Molly looked down at her plate, trying not to respond to the question. Sam needed to come to terms with his mom dating in his own way.

From the corner of her eye, she saw him press his fork to the plate repeatedly, picking up the crumbs. "She's happy. In the end, that's all I want for her."

Molly looked up, smiling at him. "You're so sweet."

"I'm always saying that," Chris said, deadpan.

Sarah laughed. "You are, Sam. She's lucky to have you."

"Hey!" Chris said.

Sarah rolled her eyes. "You're very sweet, too and your mom is very lucky to have you." She leaned in, meeting him halfway in a brief kiss. "As am I."

"That's better," Chris said. He folded his arms on the table and looked at Sam. "Heard you were out checking John Granger's tractor."

Sam looked at Molly and gave her a mock frown. "Are you posting my activities in *The Bulletin* again?"

Now Molly rolled *her* eyes. "Right. Like I need the single ladies of Britton Bay to know your whereabouts. I fully expect Cora Lester to lecture me on my intentions toward you when I swing by tomorrow."

Cora's daughter Shannon had a huge crush on Sam, which apparently the whole town knew about. When Molly had arrived, she'd met Cora at the bakery by way of Cora telling her that she was breaking her poor daughter's heart.

Sam, finished with his pie, pulled Molly against his side. He leaned in, his lips brushing over her hair. "You're the only one that matters, babe."

Her heart did that tumble thing again, and she wondered if that would fade over time.

Sam looked back at Chris. "It wasn't anything major. Why?"

"Just wondering if it was part of the vandalism he's been struggling with. Not even sure if I'd call it that. Just stuff getting moved and messed up. Things disappearing or showing up in places he didn't leave them."

"Nothing came of it the last time you followed up with him?" Sam pushed his plate away.

"No. I'm wondering if maybe it's Teddy's friends goofing around. They're about seventeen and we've picked them up a couple times for loitering and being a little too boisterous after hours on the beach."

Molly leaned back in her seat and covered her very full belly with her hand. "Is Teddy his son?" The makeshift bed, if it could be called that, popped into her head.

"He is. The other one is only eleven, I think. Could be him, too." Chris said.

Calli came to their table. "As much as I love y'all, if you leave, I can close up and go home. Pie and drinks are on the house."

"You don't have to do that, Calli," Chris said.

"Really," Sam agreed.

Dean joined them, slinging an arm around Calli's shoulder.

"Don't have to, but I am," Calli said, leaning into her husband. Her hair was looser, coming out of its usual ponytail.

Chris held up his hands. "I won't argue then. Thank you."

"Always easier not to argue," Calli agreed. "Speaking of which, things any…calmer on set, Sarah?"

Sarah was pulling her jacket on. She paused and shrugged her shoulders. "Tiffany—she was Magnolia's assistant and is now the director— is pretty intense, too, and everyone is on edge with the murder and all. It's a weird vibe to say the least."

"Yeah, that girl has her own store of temper," Dean said.

All eyes turned his way, but it was Calli who spoke. "You know her?"

Dean nodded. "She was there when I was helping with the set. I ran out to grab something from my truck and she was arguing with a woman. Yelling at her pretty loud. Definitely has her own temper."

Chris and Sarah slid out of the booth and Molly and Sam followed so they were all standing in a sort of circle. Sam helped Molly with her jacket and she slung her purse over her shoulder, her curiosity prickling.

"Who was she arguing with?"

"Don't know. Didn't see her face. Blonde hair, fancy clothes, bright red, long nails."

Chris and Molly locked eyes and both of them spoke at the same time. "Vivien."

"She didn't have her nails on when I saw her today," Molly said, thoughts swirling.

"In her statement, she said she never visits the theater," Chris said, his voice so low she wasn't sure if anyone else heard.

"The daughter?" Sam asked.

"Yes. Something isn't adding up. Can you look into when Vivien and her brother actually flew into town? She told me she arrived the night after the murder." Molly needed to write things down to sort her thoughts.

Chris nodded. "First thing in the morning."

"Sure, would be nice to see Judd cleared," Calli said. "He's a nice man. And speaking of *that,* anyone seen Corky?"

They all said no, but Molly thought again about the Granger barn and wondered if it was possible that the problems out there weren't from teens at all.

"He'll turn up," Chris said, putting a comforting hand on Calli's shoulder.

"We should go," Sam said.

They said their goodnights and left together. The stars lit up the black sky. In the distance, Molly could see the moon glistening on the still water. At the moment, Britton Bay was quiet and calm personified. Which seemed oddly ironic for a town that had so much happening below the surface.

Chapter Seventeen

Sam had only teased Molly a little when she'd bought a rolling whiteboard earlier in the year, while she'd been trying to figure out who had killed the caterer at a wedding hosted at the bed and breakfast. Now, however, with their relationship on stronger footing, he didn't hold back.

After they had gone in and greeted Tigger, Sam said he was going to walk him. Molly hemmed and hawed for a moment.

Sam walked away into their bedroom and came back a few minutes later while Molly was still trying to decide whether to be a good dog owner and girlfriend and go on the walk with them.

Sam had pulled on a hoodie and held a brown paper bag. He passed it to her. "We'll go for a walk and you do your thing."

Brows scrunched and curiosity vibrating through her, Molly opened the bag and then tipped her head back to laugh. And laugh. Then she dug out the items in the bag.

"Those are the tools, right?" Sam grinned at her.

One Sherlock Holmes hat, a toy pipe, a toy magnifying glass, and a package of whiteboard markers. She shook her head, her heart unexpectedly full.

"You are, without a doubt, the best boyfriend ever." She set the items on the counter and wound her arms around his neck.

"I don't really like you putting yourself in danger. I wanted to put a stun gun and some pepper spray in there, too." He pulled her closer so their bodies aligned perfectly and met her halfway in a sweet, soft kiss.

"I don't want to be in danger either. I kind of like the life I'm living. But I do want to help your friend."

Sam pressed his forehead to Molly's. "I want that, too. We'll be back in a bit, okay?"

"Okay. I love you."

"I love you."

Tigger, who loved them both unabashedly, jumped from one spot to the next, pouncing back and forth with excitement.

"Okay, buddy. Let's go," Sam said, chuckling.

She didn't put on the cap or put the pipe between her teeth, but Molly did open the new pack of markers and chose black. She went to the small hallway off the entry way that housed a washer and dryer and her whiteboard. She'd wiped it clean after the last mystery.

She *should* get ready for bed. Maybe read a book to get her mind off of things, but she knew herself well enough to know that her brain wouldn't switch gears until she'd purged it of information.

In the middle of the whiteboard, she put Magnolia Sweet with a circle around the woman's name. From there, she drew lines to the most likely suspects. At least in her mind. She listed them in order of her suspicions with reasons beside each:

Debra: jealousy/Beau/did she find out he's married? Alibi is a lie.

Beau: money/anger/did he stand to inherit anything? Chris checking.

Tiffany: gets to be director, resentment over treatment/ connection to V?

Vivien: lied about being at theater and arrival, arguing with T, anger toward mom, inheritance?

Jeffrey: moves up in his mother's company, anger/resentment, inheritance?

Cora: revenge for booting her from the play? The argument. Why is she covering for Deb?

In the top left corner, Molly drew a rectangle and put Judd's name in it along with the reasons he'd been arrested.

Judd Brown: Found with the body, handkerchief under her head, history of bad blood/money owed, text messages.

Molly drew a line from "text messages" and made a note reminding herself to check into the broken locker. If her list was accurate, the people who had the easiest access to Judd's locker were Tiffany, Deb, and Beau. Was it possible one of them wrote the texts and Magnolia responded because of that? Judd didn't check his phone often so maybe he hadn't even opened up the text app. Thinking about the rigid schedule at the theater made Molly think Tiffany was the one with the most opportunity. She certainly stood to gain a lot. The play, the credit, the meetings with Magnolia's Hollywood people, whoever they were.

On the bottom right side of the board, she wrote down the things she needed to do next.

1. *Talk to Cora, ask about Deb's alibi*
2. *Confront Vivien on her timeline/flight*
3. *Speak to Tiffany about fight/relationship with V*

Until she'd done those things, she couldn't go any further. She heard the door open and close as she capped her marker. Tigger came skidding into the kitchen, making Molly laugh. She kneeled down and rubbed his floppy ears.

"Wasn't that supposed to wear you out?" His mouth flopped open as he huffed and puffed.

"You'd think, right?" Sam set his keys down on the counter and glanced up. "How long were we gone? You've filled the board."

She looked back at it as she stood up. "Haven't solved anything yet except the fact that the only person who doesn't seem to be lying is the one they've accused."

Sam pulled her into a hug. "You'll find something."

No pressure, she thought. "Hopefully tomorrow. Do you want to meet at City Hall for the council announcement? I'll be there taking photos anyway, but I wanted to hear who is running."

"I can do that. I'll see if my mom wants me to swing by and pick her up. We'll meet you there. I'm curious to know who's throwing their hat in the ring."

Molly tipped her head back. "You ever think of it?"

Sam laughed. "No. I'm good right where I am. I like cars."

Molly tried to deepen her voice. "Fast cars and sexy women?"

"What more does a man need?"

Tigger let out a low, long howl and flopped on their feet. Both of them laughed.

"Just a dog," Molly said.

Chapter Eighteen

Molly knocked on the door of Cora Lester's home hair studio with a heavy dose of guilt as her companion. She'd had Jill call and schedule Anne—Jill's mother and Sam's aunt—for a cut and color. There was every chance that Cora was going to slam the door in her face.

Other than the oval sign advertising "Cora's Coifs" at the beginning of the driveway, the house looked like several others in the area: two-story heritage design with an arched roof and a sweet front porch. A swing hung from the ceiling of the porch, moving gently in the breeze.

The door swung open and Cora's radiant smile slipped immediately upon seeing Molly.

"Oh. Hello, Molly. Can I help you?"

Molly pasted on a helpless smile, cringing inside at her own underhanded behavior. "I hope so. I know it's kind of sneaky, but I asked Jill to make me an appointment with you. I'm your three o'clock. I just can't find anyone to do my hair and everyone I talk to says you're so good at it and I understand if you want me to go, but I just had to try. You said you don't take any walk-ins and I wasn't sure if you'd entertain the thought of letting me book with you and I just wanted to look good for Katherine's party tonight, so…"

Please don't slam the door.

Cora's features moved through a myriad of emotions. Frustration, surprise, and, to Molly's delight, resignation. She gave a heavy, very audible sigh and stepped back, inviting Molly in.

"I don't like the way you went about it, but I suppose I understand. I wouldn't have booked you if you'd just called. I don't like to take new clients, especially young women who change their minds at the drop of a hat."

"Oh, thank you, Cora. I really appreciate it. So much. You know how it is when you move from a big city and there's lots of people to choose from. I just didn't want to end up with orange hair like Kelly Shumaker did after she went to Valerie at Crazy Cuts."

Cora shut the door behind Molly and laughed. "You go to a place called Crazy Cuts, what do you expect? Come on in. Does Anne know you used her name?"

Molly's blush wasn't phony. "I owe her approximately one dozen scones from Bella and dinner with Sam and me."

Cora's light, easy laugh surprised Molly. "That woman knows how to make a deal. Come on. My shop is in the back."

The house was quaint, nicely decorated with a homey feel. She wondered if Shannon had grown up in this house and if she had any siblings. Short of getting the cold shoulder and a few terse words, Molly hadn't had any interactions with Cora's daughter.

Cora's shop had one of those beaded room dividers that people used to hang in their doorways ages ago. It rattled like a wooden wind instrument as they walked through. The room was set up with one washing station and one chair. The walls were a pale pink and vintage hair advertisements had been blown up and framed. It was classy and simple.

"What do you want done?" Cora gestured to the black chair in front of an oval mirror.

Molly hung her bag on a hook she noticed on the wall and then went to the chair. "A cut. That's all. Summer is coming and it's gotten long. I just need to tidy it up with a trim."

"Oh, well, that's no trouble. Let's just have you at the sink then." She put an apron around Molly and then let her settle at the sink. She washed her hair with delicious-smelling product and Molly closed her eyes a minute, remembering how much she loved the feel of someone else washing her hair.

As she'd hoped but temporarily forgotten while her scalp was being massaged, Cora began to chatter. She started with small-scale gossip— was Bella ever going to realize how much better she was than that Callan, why did the principal at the local high school think no one knew he'd had hair implants, and how Shannon was up for the vice principal job and an absolute shoo-in.

As Cora rubbed conditioner onto Molly's long brown hair, Molly asked, "Who do you think we'll have for potential mayoral candidates?" She just needed to get her to relax into an easy conversation before pitching some harder questions.

Cora smiled down at her. "My gut is we'll only have a few. Lots of people are happy to complain about a situation, but when it comes time to step up and do something about it, make a change, we're oddly silent. I'm hoping Sheriff Saron just stays."

Molly didn't respond with what she knew. It wasn't her place to say, and everyone would know soon enough.

Cora pursed her lips a moment. "We'd do well with someone who has a history here. Someone like John Granger. But on the other hand, wouldn't hurt to have someone like Beau Harrison. He's one of us but not from here, so he's got some perspective."

Molly made an "mmm" sound, not wanting to show her happiness at the conversation leading into the perfect segue. Cora turned on the spray hose and rinsed Molly's hair.

"I wonder if Debra has any thoughts on Beau running. She doesn't seem like she enjoys sharing his attention all that much," Molly said, eyes closed.

She didn't need her eyes open to feel the way Cora's fingers tightened in her hair. "Yes, well, that woman doesn't know a good thing when she sees it. She doesn't deserve him."

Molly's eyelids fluttered open. "Oh? I thought you were friends."

Cora scoffed and pulled a towel off a shelf above her. Molly saw the tense set of her jaw. "No. We're not friends. She doesn't know how to have friends. Or a boyfriend. Thinks bribing and conniving is the way to people's hearts."

As she sat up, wincing a little when Cora's towel drying got a bit rough, Molly said, "I'm sorry. I didn't realize that. I chatted with her the other day. She said she'd been with you during the time of the murder."

Cora's hands stopped and her breathing hitched. Molly's heart did the same. "What are you really doing here, Molly?"

Cora stepped away as Molly stood, holding the towel to her head. "I really do need a haircut. But the truth is, Judd didn't kill Magnolia. We can't let him go to jail while the real killer goes free."

The hairdresser's already pale face went completely ashen. "But Chris arrested Judd."

"Yes. There was a lot of convenient evidence. And other people had alibis. Ones that may not have been true. For instance, Deb wasn't with you when she said she was, was she?"

Cora turned away. Approaching a multi-drawer storage unit, she started pulling things out: scissors, comb, clips. "I don't know where you heard that."

"Cora, if Beau or Deb are guilty, that's going to come to light. I truly believe you really *can't* get away with murder."

Cora dropped a couple of the clips on the ground and when she straightened from picking them up, she met Molly's gaze. "Beau is a good man. Deb is always worrying about him cheating but I don't know why. It's plain as day he loves her. He is a *good* man, Molly. Not a murderer."

Before bringing up the fact that Cora only spoke on behalf of Beau, Molly said, "So is Judd." The more she dug into this, the more she believed it.

Cora swallowed, her eyes darting away. "Deb has a heck of a temper. You think Magnolia was something, you should see Deb when she doesn't get what she wants."

"Enough of a temper to kill? Why did you cover for her?"

The hairdresser looked down. Molly stepped forward. "Are you scared of her?"

Cora's head snapped up. "Good lord, no. I'm embarrassed is all. Being taken for a fool doesn't feel nice. She told me she'd help me get a bigger role in the play. They've had to do some shuffling and Tiffany is taking out some of the ridiculous ideas Magnolia added to the script. A tree. Like I want to be a tree?"

Really? She'd covered for a possible murderer to get a better role? Molly thought she'd left Hollywood, but maybe not.

Cora gestured to the chair in front of the mirror. "Sit down. I have another appointment in a half hour."

Molly sat. "Why did Deb ask you to cover for her?"

"Because she was following Beau. She came to me, said she didn't want him to know she didn't trust him all the way and the cops had asked where she was. She said it was the first thing that popped into her mind."

Was it because Deb had been too frazzled from being asked her whereabouts? Or maybe she'd felt guilty and hadn't thought things all the way through to having an alibi.

Cora started talking about the play and opening night, the buzz surrounding it, and how people on set were arguing over Tiffany's insistence that one of them open with an "ode to Magnolia."

"I mean, if she loves the woman so much, why not just say something herself?"

Molly didn't respond because she was too wrapped up in her own thoughts. If she had to put her suspects in order right this minute, she'd go with

1. Deb—jealousy was a powerful motivator

2. Tiffany/Vivien—money was also a powerful motivator, as was success, plus they clearly knew each other

3. ~~Beau~~—lied about alibi/golf

Cora could be crossed off. Not only did she not strike Molly as a killer—gut instinct was about all she had at the moment—but she didn't have enough to gain. In the time Molly had lived in Britton Bay, she'd experienced Cora's unkind words, cold shoulder, and dismissal. She'd never seen evidence of aggression or violence. Which didn't necessarily mean anything, but again, Cora had nothing to gain by Magnolia's death, and in her experience, murder was usually committed for a reason.

Though she wanted to talk to him again, she also felt fairly confident about crossing Beau off of her list. He'd known the woman for years, married her, *lived* with her. If he hadn't killed her then, why would he now?

She sent Chris a quick text and asked about the will and Vivien's arrival in case he forgot. He wouldn't, but she really needed that information.

If Beau stood to inherit nothing, he had no motive. Unless…what if he wanted to marry Deb and Magnolia wouldn't divorce him? Why were they still married after all of these years? If Beau was about to inherit millions, maybe he did have a reason. But why now? Did he suddenly need money?

Okay. Maybe he wasn't all the way crossed off. When Molly left Cora's, happy with her hair and satisfied with her decision to take the woman off her suspect list, she tried to put all thoughts of the murder and Magnolia out of her head. Tonight was about celebrating a very special woman.

Chapter Nineteen

"What a lovely way to spend my birthday evening. Thank you," Katherine said as they loaded into her car.

Molly sat up front with Katherine, then turned in her seat. "You could have the front, you know. Your legs are a little longer than mine."

"I'm good. Glad you enjoyed dinner, Mom," Sam said from the back, winking at Molly.

Katherine pulled out of the parking lot of the Greek restaurant they'd chosen, about a half hour outside of Britton Bay. Molly glanced back to make sure Sam was texting Brandon and Calli to let them know they were on their way. Once they were on the highway, music playing softly in the background, Katherine glanced in her rear view at Sam.

"I hope you don't mind, but I've invited Brandon over for dessert tonight. I asked him to come around eight. I have some of Bella's new peanut butter squares," Katherine said.

Sam sat forward, resting a hand on his mom's shoulder. "He's part of your life, Mom. I don't mind at all. Though I *would* mind if we didn't have birthday cake to celebrate. Molly and I picked one up."

His mom looked over at Molly. "You two didn't have to do that."

"It's your birthday. Of course we did," Molly said.

"I'm a very lucky woman," Katherine said.

The ride home was uneventful, but butterflies swirled in Molly's stomach. They'd been working for weeks on this surprise, and with the way news slid through the town, she was shocked they'd managed to keep it quiet. She hoped that everyone was there and that they'd had no trouble setting up. They hadn't been given a huge window. After Molly had returned from Cora's, she'd tried to convince Katherine that they should go do some shopping before dinner just to give their friends more time, but Katherine had just wanted to sit on the deck with her and Tigger and said there was no reason to bring Sam home early from work.

Here we go, she thought as Katherine pulled into her driveway. It wasn't by accident that Sam had told her to take the route that led to the back of the house instead of the front. He'd said Chris had texted about an accident, and suggested an alternate road that would keep the cars and twinkle lights out front a surprise to the last minute.

"What a gorgeous night," Katherine said as they got out of the car. She started for the back deck.

"Let's go sit on the front porch and wait for Brandon," Sam said.

Katherine stopped in her tracks and stared at her son. "Are you suddenly missing him?" Her lips tipped up in a smile and her gaze shimmered with amusement in the dusky evening.

"It's a nice night to sit on the porch. You and Molly got to do it earlier. Come on," Sam said, holding a hand out for her.

Molly bit the inside of her lip and followed behind them. When Sam turned his head to make eye contact, she mouthed, "Subtle."

"What?" The word and Katherine's breath whooshed out as the large white canopy shining with twinkle lights came into view when they rounded the side of the house.

Katherine looked back at Molly and then at Sam as a couple dozen people stepped out of the shadows and yelled "Surprise!" At the front was Brandon, wearing jeans and a button-down shirt along with his heart on his sleeve, holding a gorgeous bouquet of the yellowest flowers Molly had ever seen.

Her hands flew to her mouth as she took in the surroundings. Their friends and family had used the time well. Pots of flowers lined the edges of the tent, music played from outdoor speakers, a few tables and several chairs had been set up, and a Happy Birthday sign hung from one pole to another over a dessert table that held not only an array of delicious treats but Bella's three-tiered masterpiece.

Brandon stepped forward and passed the flowers to Katherine, love shining in his eyes. "Happy birthday, sweetheart."

She threw her arms around him, crushing the flowers between them then pulled back with a laugh and did the same to Molly and Sam.

"I can't believe you guys did all of this," she cried when she stepped back, tears sliding down her cheeks.

"Come on, don't cry, Mom. Of course we did this. It's your birthday. We love you." Sam pulled her close for another hug.

"We do," Brandon said.

He and Sam locked gazes and Molly slipped her hand into her boyfriend's, proud of him and happy for Katherine when her son nodded, a genuine smile on his face.

"Let's get this party started," Calli called, coming over to hug Katherine.

It was the first of dozens of hugs as people surged forward to greet her and say, "Happy Birthday."

Molly did a brief walk around, making sure that everyone had drinks and the presents were all on one table, and saying hello to the guests. Though Katherine was loved by what seemed like the whole town, Sam and Brandon had taken care of the guest list, inviting mostly just close friends and family.

A few couples started to dance fairly early into the evening and Molly settled on the sidelines, truly enjoying the laughter and chatting, the music, and the sweet energy emanating from inside and outside the large white canopy tent.

Jill came up beside her, passing her a glass of punch. "You guys did an excellent job."

Molly grinned at her friend. "It was definitely a group effort. Any trouble getting everything set up?"

Jill shook her head. "Nope. Went off without a hitch. Usually things like this do though when you've got so many hands."

"I need to introduce myself to your mom, but I'm still feeling a bit guilty about operation haircut."

Her friend's loud laughter turned eyes their way, including Sam's. He was chatting with his mom and a couple that Molly didn't recognize.

"You'll get your chance. She's over there by the desserts chatting with Bella. And also, that cake is amazing. Why don't we go take a closer look and I'll introduce you now? I promise she's not scary."

Instead of waiting for an answer, Jill looped her arm through Molly's and tugged her toward the dessert table. Since they'd known they were taking Katherine out for dinner to get her away from the bed and breakfast, they'd agreed to do a dessert bar instead of appetizers and such. As much as Molly wanted to sample every treat on the table, now seemed like a bad time since she really didn't want to face Sam's aunt.

Too bad. Jill stopped in front of a dark-haired woman, about the same height as Molly. She wore a flower-patterned sundress and a light pink sweater over top. Though she was only Katherine's sister-in-law, they resembled each other in the fact that neither of them looked anywhere near their age.

"Ahh. The infamous Molly Owens," Anne said, setting a bite-sized cookie down on the plate she was holding. "Editor of the newspaper, catcher of my nephew's heart, puppy rescuer, crime solver, and undercover hair operative."

Molly burst out laughing, all of her nerves fluttering away on the evening breeze. "I see my reputation precedes me."

"That it does, my dear. That it does. It's nice to finally meet you. I'm Anne, as you know. And this is my husband, Don," she said as a tall, gray-haired man joined them.

They shook hands and chatted about everything with an ease that shouldn't have surprised Molly. Since the minute she'd driven into this town, almost everyone had been friendly and welcoming to her. Spending an evening with these people could make an outsider feel like they'd been around forever.

When Sam wandered over a few minutes later, greeting his aunt and uncle, they excused themselves and went to dance. Sam grinned down at Molly.

"Are you having fun?" He looped his arm around her shoulder as they stood on the edge of the makeshift dance floor.

Molly leaned her head into the crook of his arm. "I am. You did good."

Sam turned his head and pressed a kiss to Molly's forehead. "I'd say we all did."

She was about to ask him if he wanted to dance when Sarah and Chris wandered over. Sarah was dressed in a pretty floor-length dress the color of the sky with a white cardigan over it. Chris looked relaxed in jeans and a button-down shirt. Molly pressed her hand to Sam's chest, learning closer into him.

"Nice party," Chris said, his hand linked with Sarah's.

"It turned out great. Mom is thrilled. Thanks for all your help. The sign looks great, Sarah," Sam said.

She glanced over at it. The huge letters were painted in bright colors with cupcakes and presents around the border. "Thanks. It turned out well. I can't wait to get into that cake."

They laughed and Molly agreed. She looked up at Sam. "We'll let people mingle and dance a while longer and then sing to her?"

"Sounds good. Doesn't look like anyone is in a rush." He gestured with his chin toward Brandon leading his mother onto the dance floor, a dreamy look in Katherine's eyes.

"One by one, all the single men in this town are disappearing," Jill said as she and Bella joined them. She pointed between the two couples and then gestured to the paired-up dancers. "We're going to have to scout men from other towns. Oh, wait, Molly already started doing that for some of us."

Jill snickered and gave Bella a little shoulder shove. Bella's cheeks turned bright red.

Sam's grip loosened around her shoulders and he looked down at her. "Something I should know, babe? Matchmaking on the side of all the other things?"

Molly shook her head, sending Jill a narrow-eyed glare. "*No.* I hired Gavin and that's it. Well, I also talked to a couple of other candidates, two from the University of Portland and they're coming up for interviews and both male so...hmmm...maybe I am scouting single men."

They all laughed, Bella included. Chris glanced at Molly. "Gavin? That's the waiter from last week?"

Jill answered for her with an emphatic nod. "Yup. He's a cutie. And a good writer."

Bella looked down at the ground. Jill nudged her with her hip. "And he has good taste. Seems he's already addicted to Bella's goodies."

The baker's head snapped up and she glared at Jill, then looked at the others. "He likes the baked goods. That's what my former friend means."

Putting an arm around her shoulder, Jill hugged her friend close. "Aw. Don't be like that. I just want you to be happy. With or without a guy, but if it's with one, I want him to deserve you."

The quiet lull raised the question of where Callan was. Bella sighed. "I think I'm just fine being single. If you think Gavin's so cute, maybe you should ask him out."

That solved one mystery: Bella and Callan were broken up.

"Nah. Not my type. No workplace romances for me," Jill said.

The subject shifted as they chatted about any and all topics that had nothing to do with what had been on everyone's minds. It was a nice reprieve from discussions about murder, but when Chris caught Molly's gaze, her shoulders stiffened.

"Are police officers allowed to dance with newspaper editors?" she asked, hoping the joke would keep everyone else's mind away from where both of theirs had clearly landed.

"As long as said newspaper editor isn't stepping on my toes—literally, this time—it shouldn't be a problem. That okay, babe?" Chris kissed Sarah's cheek.

"Of course. When you're ready for someone to step on your feet, just call me over," Sarah said.

Everyone laughed but Chris leaned down and whispered to her, loud enough for Molly to hear. "*You can step on my feet any time.*"

Sarah grinned up at him as he kissed her before taking Molly's hand and pulling her onto the dance floor.

"You guys are a great couple," Molly said as she placed her hands on his shoulders. The slow song made it easy to talk and move. She wasn't a bad dancer; she just didn't have much opportunity to do it.

"We are. I want to ask her to move in with me," Chris said, his eyes staring over Molly's shoulder, likely at the girl in question.

"What's stopping you? If you say it's too soon, I'll tell you the one thing I've learned is that someone else's timeline of when things are appropriate doesn't matter. If it feels right, you do it."

Chris met her gaze, held it for a moment. "It's not that. I don't care what anyone else thinks. And I love her. But it's not easy living with a cop. I work long hours, have to leave in the middle of the night sometimes. Until recently crime hasn't been a huge issue, but the things that come up, especially lately, can take their toll. After a particularly rough shift, I'm not always in the best mood, and I'd hate to come home and take that out on her."

Molly smiled. She wasn't the only person who'd moved to town and found a good man. "Talk to her. She loves you and knows what she's getting into. She moved here all by herself, away from her family, and started her own successful business. She's shy but she isn't afraid to share her opinion. If she doesn't want to, she'll say so."

"You're fairly smart when you're not annoying me."

Molly grinned and squeezed his shoulder. "Same. So?"

He didn't even pretend not to know what she wanted. He pulled her the slightest bit closer. "Beau inherits nothing. Everything goes to the kids, with the lion's share going to Vivien. No clue why it's not split equally among the kids. Vivien flew in four days before the murder. She was probably already staying at her mother's house when it happened."

"So she lied about several things."

Chris nodded. "Definitely. She and Tiffany know each other from L.A. Vivien is in charge of hiring for her mother. Whether or not they knew each other before the play, I don't know. But Vivien was the one who sent Tiffany out here to be Magnolia's assistant."

Molly pulled her bottom lip between her teeth, digesting that information. "They could have been working together. Were there fingerprints on Magnolia's neck? Like could you tell if she was strangled by a man or a woman?"

Chris's jaw tightened. Molly knew it was hard for him to share details that weren't supposed to be public knowledge. The fact that he was doing so spoke to how much he believed in Judd.

He shook his head and leaned in, putting his mouth closer to her ear. "No. She was strangled with some sort of fabric. Not sure what. They're testing the fibers they found. But a tox screen showed she had sedatives in her system."

Someone had drugged her beforehand? To make it easier to kill her? That seemed so strange. Or maybe it was smart. Molly wasn't sure since it was hard to think like a killer.

The song was winding down. "Anything else?"

"Yeah," Chris said, his voice low. "Beau filed paperwork for a divorce on the day she was murdered. He brought them into city hall and they timestamped them. Three forty-two."

Molly had already been at the theater by then. And Magnolia had already been dead. It wasn't Beau. So, what was he hiding?

The song stopped and Molly stepped back while blinking several times, her brain spinning. Before another song could start, Sam's arm wrapped around her from behind.

"Time for cake," he said, loud enough for everyone to hear. As the guests and Katherine moved toward the table, he whispered in her ear, "It can wait, babe. Whatever it is that has your brain turning, we can talk about it later."

Molly turned in his arms and smiled up at him. "You're right. Of course. Let's sing to your mom."

They joined the others as Bella lit the candles. Molly told herself to focus on the moment, being part of this celebration and this family. But in the back of her mind, she thought about Magnolia's family and wondered if instead of celebrating her, one of them had killed her instead.

Chapter Twenty

The newspaper was closed on Sundays, and Molly and Sam typically took the day for themselves. They often tried new activities that one of them enjoyed. Sam teased her that he'd introduced her to kayaking, paddle boarding, and changing a tire while Molly had taught him how to break and enter and host a stakeout.

She wasn't sure what today would include, but at some point she needed to find a way to talk to Vivien. Soon. The woman was hiding behind at least two lies, and it was time to find out why. But first, she wanted a little intel on the Hollywood family and she knew just the person.

She left Sam and Tigger to sleep—the spoiled dog had curled into Sam's side as soon as Molly had roused herself. In the kitchen, she sent a text to her friend from California, asking if she was awake enough to chat. While she waited for a response, she made coffee and tried to think of the last time she'd spoken to Tori.

They'd met in L.A. when Tori had put out a request for an editor. As a successful scriptwriter, she'd needed assistance more than once, and she and Molly had even worked on a few things together. Molly still received royalties for the commercial script she and Tori had written. Between their working together and Molly hardly knowing anyone in California, having followed a guy out there, she and Tori had become friends. She was the only thing Molly missed about living there.

Her phone buzzed at the same time as the coffee began to percolate.

Tori: Not only am I awake, I haven't gone to sleep. If you don't mind sleep-deprived slurring, dial away.

Molly laughed and phoned her friend. Instead of a greeting, she said, "Why didn't you go to sleep? Out partying with celebrities?"

Tori yawned loudly and chuckled. "That would be so much cooler than the truth. I had a deadline and writer's block which, as you know, don't mix. I was up all night working on a comedy sketch I'm pitching this afternoon."

Molly leaned on the counter, watching the coffee drip. "Tor, that's awesome. Did you finish?"

"Barely. It's done but it's rough. If I hadn't been so busy all month, I would have finished earlier and sent you a draft to look over. It'll have to do though. It's an informal meeting. I'll be talking them through the show. The script is basically just a prop and a snapshot. As long as I can get some sleep first, I should be able to pitch it well."

"You will. I have no doubt. How's everything else? When are you going to come see me?"

"I like your confidence in me. Everything is good. The same. I'm dating one of the writers from *The Four of Us*," she said, mentioning a hit television show. "He's pretty great. So far."

Molly laughed, walking to the cupboard to grab coffee mugs. "So far? Waiting for the other shoe to drop?"

"Come on. Doesn't it always?"

Molly glanced back at the bedroom door as it opened and Sam shuffled out, Tigger at his heels.

"I used to think so, but not anymore. Not when it's right."

"Oh my goodness. You sound like a mushy chick flick."

Sam pressed a kiss to her cheek and poured them both coffees.

"I know. It feels good."

"It sounds good on you, Mol. As to the visiting, if I get this gig, I'll need to write several episodes. No reason I can't do that at the bed and breakfast I've heard so much about."

Molly's heart jumped with excitement. She smiled at Sam when he slid the coffee toward her on the counter and mouthed "thank you." He nodded, took his coffee and went to the back door with Tigger. The deck wasn't entirely finished, but they'd set a couple of folding chairs out there.

"You absolutely should," Molly said. "I miss you and would love to see you."

"Me too. I'll see what I can do. So, what's up? Why are we communicating in this ancient and archaic way?"

With a laugh, Molly picked up her coffee. "I wanted to ask if you knew anything about Magnolia Sweet and her children. I figure it's a long shot but thought I'd ask."

"Not such a long shot actually. It's a lot of what I've heard through the grapevine and read in tabloids, but I know a few things firsthand as well."

Molly padded out to the deck where Sam was staring out into the yard and Tigger was jumping around like a rabbit. She sat beside him and his free hand immediately came to her thigh. She smiled at the contact. They sat like that as Molly listened to Tori filling her in on what she knew—she'd obviously heard about the murder—and after making promises to talk soon, she hung up.

"Good morning," Sam said, looking at her.

"Back at you. You sleep okay?" She sipped her coffee, biting back a sigh of pleasure at the delicious taste.

"I did. Until you left. I sleep better with you beside me," Sam said, his voice still a little rough from waking up.

"I didn't think you'd notice," Molly said, looking over with a cheeky smile. "I left a perfectly good substitute."

Sam chuckled and looked at Tigger. "He's way hairier and a total bed hog. Definitely not a good substitute."

Tigger trotted over and whined to jump up on Sam's lap. When he was told no, he sulked and lay across Sam's bare feet.

"Was that Tori you were talking to?"

The scent of dewy flowers surrounded them. Molly looked forward to many mornings like this, though there was a slight chill in the air. "It was. I asked her about Magnolia. I'd heard that she had left L.A. under interesting circumstances but couldn't find anything online about it for certain."

"And Tori knew the reason?"

Shrugging, Molly lowered her mug to her lap. "Rumors, but insider ones if that counts. Magnolia had started her own production company, which I knew, but what I didn't know was that no one would work with her. That's why Vivien and Jeffrey are in charge there. Magnolia threw an enormous fit on some bigwig. The woman told Magnolia that as long as she was the head of the company, she'd get no work in Hollywood. So, Vivien and Jeffrey convinced her to come home. Reap the rewards of their hard work that she'd paved the way for. Apparently, Vivien is much like her mother in the savvy department but less socially abrasive."

"How about the son? What's his role?"

"From what I've read and heard? Rich playboy. I honestly think he does a lot of the wining and dining. He definitely strikes me as someone who knows how to schmooze. And I hate that word but it applies."

She laughed when Sam said the word a couple of times like he was trying it out. "You're right, it's a weird word. He fits the profile for playboy, but how about murderer?"

She shook her head. "I don't think so. I need to talk to Beau and Debra today to rule them out, but my gut is telling me Tiffany and Vivien are hiding a lot more than we think. I'm hoping we can swing by the set today. I know they're having a big dress rehearsal since the play opens in a week."

Sam set his coffee cup down, then took Molly's from her grasp, ignoring her protest, and set it on the deck as well. Then he took her hand and tugged her over to his lap. For a moment, he just held her, his arms wrapped around her. Any arguments she had slipped from her mind as she melted into him. Tigger, not one to waste an opportunity, immediately bounded up and settled in Molly's chair, scaring himself when it wobbled.

Molly laughed. "You're okay, buddy." He curled into a ball and closed his eyes.

Sam stroked a hand along her arm, to her fingers, his running over the lingering bruise from Judd's harsh grip. "It's your turn to choose a Sunday activity. Rehearsal doesn't sound like much fun, but it's your pick."

She kissed him and pressed her forehead to his. "That's not my pick. Just a small piece of our day."

"Okay. But fair warning, I'm looking into boxing for my pick. At least then I'll know you'll know how to defend yourself." His tone was teasing and light, but she knew he worried.

"There's no danger, Sam."

"Yet. No danger, yet."

"Believe it or not, I don't plan on finding any."

He kissed her, his hand drifting up into her hair. When he pulled back, his eyes were more awake. "You don't have to plan on something for it to show up."

Chapter Twenty-One

Before heading to the theater Sam and Molly enjoyed a homestyle breakfast with his mom, who was still glowing with happiness from her party the night before. If it bothered Sam that Brandon was already there, cooking breakfast with Katherine, he didn't let it show. It seemed he was finally coming to terms with his mother's relationship. Molly knew it wasn't so much about his mother dating as it was about his father being gone. She could tell it pleased Katherine greatly when her two favorite guys got into a heated but friendly debate over vehicles.

They drove to the recreation center, and Molly's stomach cramped as soon as they turned into the parking lot. It was strange, in her mind, how she could look for clues and puzzle pieces, but the minute she returned to the scene, it was like her body and brain reminded her of what she'd been trying to block out. Namely, the images that came hard and fast as soon as Sam turned off his truck.

"You okay?"

She swallowed the lump in her throat. "Yes. I'm good. I'm going to take the most direct route with Beau and Deb that I can."

Sam opened his door but paused. "I think Chris should be doing this."

"You know they can't waste resources on digging into something that the department considers solved."

They got out of the truck and met around the front, reaching for each other's hands at the same time.

"Maybe that's true," Sam said. "But he could be asking questions on his own."

Molly sent him a sideways glance as they walked. "You think that won't put people on guard if a cop is asking the questions instead? Especially when people are feeling relatively safe, thinking they know who the murderer is."

"At least you're not on your own," Sam said.

She didn't point out that there'd be an entire cast there along with him. Instead, she just squeezed his hand and went first when he held the door open for her. The guy at the reception desk looked like a teenager with his spotty facial hair and crooked smile.

"Morning," he greeted, stacking clipboards.

"Morning. We're just here to check out the play," Molly said, pulling her press badge out just in case. "I heard the director is doing a final dress rehearsal today."

It never hurt to feed random people that sort of information because Molly found it often got them talking.

The teen didn't even glance at the press lanyard. "Sure. It's right down the hall and through the double doors. Pretty sure they're rehearsing." He shrugged and continued with his task.

Molly and Sam walked into the rehearsal to find it in full swing and at the end of the production. They sat patiently as Dorothy finally arrived home to the safe and loving arms of Auntie Em and Uncle Henry.

What surprised Molly was that when the play was clearly over and the spotlight shone on Dorothy, no one yelled 'cut' or applauded. Instead, Cora, dressed in a monkey costume with wings, stepped to center stage.

"Okay. We need to all file off and then come back for our bows the way we practiced," Cora said.

"You're not in charge just because Tiffany had to leave, Cora," Debra said, stepping away from embracing the girl playing Dorothy.

"But she's right," the girl said. "The audience will be clapping, the curtain closes and then we file off, curtain opens, we come back on."

Beau reached for Debra's hand and then looked out into the audience. "Jim, can you close the curtains and open them again so we can practice?"

"You got it, Beau," a voice said through the speakers.

The curtain began to close and Molly leaned over to Sam. The theater was dark with the stage lights shielded by the curtain.

"Tiffany isn't here. That seems odd," Molly said.

"It does seem weird. Maybe she had some things she had to do," Sam whispered.

The curtain opened and as the cast walked out, ensemble groups like the monkeys first, Molly and Sam clapped. It took several minutes to go through the cast before Dorothy walked onto the stage and took the spotlight. She bowed, then stepped back so the rest of the cast could join hands and bow together.

There was laughter and excited chatter when the last bow was taken. Beau saw Sam and Molly and walked to the edge of the stage as people high fived and began going in different directions.

"You got another sneak peek," Beau said, looking at Molly.

The house lights came up, momentarily blinding everyone. Jim, the guy in the sound booth, came back on the speaker. "Half-hour break and we go again, everyone."

"It's going to be great. I'm so impressed with everyone's professionalism in light of how rough things have been," Molly said.

She and Sam stood and wandered closer to the stage. Molly saw Deb watching them from the side.

"We pull together. We're a family," Beau said. He glanced back at Debra, then turned his gaze to Molly and Sam again. His smile looked forced.

"Where's Tiffany?" Sam asked.

Shock crossed Beau's features, like that hadn't been the question he was expecting. "Oh. She, uh, I don't know actually. She got a text and said she had an emergency and had to go. Said she'd be back for the second round."

The stage was starting to clear out. It looked so fun and enchanting; it was hard to believe there'd been a dead body on it not that long ago.

"Beau? We need to take a rest before the next round," Deb called.

Molly waved at her then addressed Beau. "Actually, could I talk to you both for a quick second?"

Even though she kept her tone even, Molly's pulse doubled. Deb came over, her gait stiff and obviously reluctant. As if by silent agreement, no one said anything until Deb and Beau came down the stage steps and the rest of the cast cleared off.

Beau and Deb both switched off their microphones, which Molly found interesting and somewhat telling. They certainly didn't want to broadcast anything.

"We don't have a lot of time, Molly. What do you want?" Deb linked her fingers with Beau's.

Beau's mouth tightened and he looked down at Deb. "Deb. Be nice."

She let out a huff. "Right. Now that you want to be mayor we have to put up with abuse from the public?"

Whoa. Cora was right.

"You're running?" Sam asked.

Beau stood straighter. "I am. That's not public knowledge until tomorrow though, if you don't mind."

"Of course," Molly said. "Then it's actually good that we showed up now to settle something before you begin campaigning."

"Settle what?" Deb's voice went up an octave.

Glancing around to make sure there was no one hovering, Molly didn't hold back. They didn't have time. Any of them.

"You both lied about your whereabouts to the police. Beau, I'm pretty much one hundred percent positive you were busy at the time of the murder, but Deb, where were you, really?"

Debra's jaw dropped and Beau made a strange noise in the back of his throat. Sam put his arm around Molly's waist, drawing her closer to his side.

"You awful woman. How dare you accuse me of lying?"

Molly ignored her outrage. "Better me than the police. While I don't know if Beau has shared his whereabouts with you, his time has been accounted for by the sheriff very recently. Not where he claimed to be, but it rules him out. You, however, are hiding something."

"Why are you doing this, Molly?" Beau's voice was even and soft.

Sam cleared his throat. "Judd Brown is a good man. He didn't kill Magnolia. We want to know who did."

Molly smiled up at Sam, appreciating him as much in that moment as she loved him. She looked back at Beau. "I'm not trying to out your secrets, especially from each other, but Judd matters to Sam and a lot of people in this town. We're just trying to help him."

Beau shifted uncomfortably while Deb crossed her arms over her chest. "I was getting my hair done."

"No, you weren't. I spoke to Cora," Molly said.

Beau looked at Deb. "Where were you, honey?"

"Where were *you?*" Deb countered, glaring at him.

Beau brushed a hand through his hair and sighed. "I was at City Hall submitting a petition to divorce."

Debra stepped back. "You were?"

"Where did you think I was?" Beau moved closer to her. "Where were *you?*"

Tears sprang to Deb's eyes. "I was parked outside of Magnolia's house, certain I'd catch you two coming out of it before she left for the theater."

"Deb. You thought I was cheating on you?" Beau's voice sounded anguished.

"Only one of us was your wife," Deb said, the bite of her words losing their heat with her wobbly voice.

Beau took her by the shoulders. "That's because she fought me on it. But I finally convinced her a few weeks ago to sign the damn papers. So I could ask *you* to marry me."

Debra's hand flew to her mouth and Sam and Molly exchanged a glance.

"What? I'd seen the two of you coming out of her office backstage and you looked…rattled. I thought she'd asked you to get back together. To start things up again."

"She did. I told her no. I told her I was in love with you and that if she didn't sign the papers, I'd quit the play. She didn't want any obstacles in her path to showing Hollywood that she could succeed in a small town as easily as there."

Deb threw her arms around him and Molly and Sam stepped back, giving them a moment to chat. Or cry, in Deb's case. Beau smoothed his hand down her hair and murmured as they hugged each other tight.

"Guess that rules them out," Sam whispered in her ear.

Beau shifted Deb so his arm was around her. "Obviously we both had our reasons for keeping secrets." He looked at Deb. "Which we'll need to not do in the future." She nodded and sniffled.

Beau smiled at her and Deb's entire presence softened. He looked back at Sam and Molly. "It'd mean a lot if you two could keep this to yourselves. Except for, you know, sharing with the sheriff that we aren't murderers."

Molly nodded, feeling a strange twist of embarrassment, happiness for them, and nerves. The list was narrowing.

"Of course. We'll see you tomorrow at City Hall," Molly said.

"But wait," Deb said as they started to walk away. "If Judd really didn't do it, that means there's still a killer on the loose. And it might be someone we know."

Chapter Twenty-Two

City Hall was an impressive brick and cement building with mountain-high doors and a gorgeous clock in the center of the peaked roof. It was around the block from the police station and surrounded by what Molly would have termed the "business district." Instead of quaint shops and yummy eateries, the buildings in this area had a more specific function. City Hall, the police department, the school board office, and the fire hall were all clustered close together. Molly often thought *The Bulletin* would be better suited to this area, but Alan's grandfather had purchased their building before Main Street had become what it was today.

The parking lot was nearly full by the time Jill and Molly, who'd driven together in Jill's car, arrived. People wanted to know who their mayoral candidates were and what promises they had in store for the town. But those who'd been hoping for Brandon Saron to be their mayor were going to be sorely disappointed.

Molly waved to several people—local business owners, friends, and people she knew in passing. She and Jill weaved through the crowd toward the steps that led up to the entrance.

"Any thoughts on who the potentials will be?" Jill asked.

Molly held the camera close to her chest and shook her head. None she could share. "Nope. I think there's probably a lot of long-time business owners who could step up."

They'd just about reached the door when Molly saw something from the corner of her eye. Was that…?

"I'll be right back. Can you take this for me?" She lifted the camera off of her neck and passed it to Jill.

Jill's puzzled expression didn't stop her from taking the camera and slipping the strap over her own neck. "Sure. You okay?"

Stopping in the path forced people to move around them. Molly apologized, already trying to move against the human tide. "Yeah. Take pictures if I can't get back in, okay?"

Jill waved and went into the building while Molly muttered "excuse me" and "sorry" a dozen times as she went back down the stairs.

She went to the left of the building, which was lined with trees and a cobblestone path that Molly knew led to a little garden with a small pond. Corky was walking quickly, like a man on a mission, his head down. His shoulders were hunched. She called his name, and saw him shake his head and keep walking.

"Corky? It's Molly," she called again.

He stopped. He didn't turn around, but he waited for her to approach. She could see from the way his shoulders shifted back and forth that he was rubbing his hands together. He did it when he was nervous. Corky Templeton was an enigma. At times, he seemed entirely in his own world. He was loved and cared for by the town, but he was very selective with what he'd accept help for. He wouldn't stay with anyone who offered him a home, but he frequented Calli's and Bella's for food. He wouldn't take money, but he always accepted coffee. No one knew if he had any family in the area—or at all.

Molly approached, her footfalls gentle, and came up around him, giving him a wide berth as sometimes he startled easily.

"Hi Corky."

His worn and torn canvas jacket fit loose on his shoulders. Molly wondered if he'd lost weight. His graying hair was matted and thick, but his brown eyes were cognizant and friendly.

"Hi Molly."

She smiled at him as she put her hands in her pockets. "Were you just checking out who is running for mayor?"

He nodded, glancing left and right before focusing on her again. He'd been a little harder to have a conversation with since he'd found the body of a celebrity chef at the end of summer.

"Sheriff Saron is a good man. He's a nice man. Sam, too. Your Sam is a nice man."

"They are, you're right." She slid a little closer, keeping her body as still as possible. Unsure how he'd respond, she went with her hunch. "Do you like kittens, Corky?"

His lips burst into a wide smile. Despite living on the street, he usually kept up a decent appearance, including having all of his teeth. Molly knew the homeless situation in Britton Bay and the surrounding area was an uphill struggle, and in comparison, Corky fared better than many.

"They're so soft. They love me," Corky said.

Molly moved a little closer, hands still in her pockets. "Of course they do."

His eyes widened and he leaned into her. "How's Tigger?"

When Molly had found her pup, he'd been homeless, like Corky. "He's getting so big. You can come visit him at the bed and breakfast."

Corky shook his head vehemently. "No. Nope. No, thank you. I need to go now."

"Corky, everyone is worried about you. Calli and Bella have missed you. Where are you staying?"

Corky started fidgeting with his hands and looking around. "Calli and Bella are nice."

"They are. Do you want to say hi to them? Calli would love to see you."

"No, thank you. I have to go."

"Can I give you a ride somewhere?" *Like maybe a place with an overload of kittens?*

"No. I like to walk. I have to go now. Bye, Molly."

She didn't want to upset him or push him, but she definitely planned on following up her theory. As soon as she found out who else was planning on trying to be mayor of their little town.

* * * *

While Jill took the camera and the pictures of their three mayoral hopefuls back to *The Bulletin*, Molly caught up with Sam, who'd ended up coming separately from his mom. That worked out well for Molly. Walking hand in hand toward his truck, she wondered if Corky was currently making the long trek back to the Granger farm. *If* she was right about that, he probably was.

"You might not know the candidates well, still being new, but they're all top notch," Sam said when they got in his truck.

"Do you have a favorite?" Molly asked.

He ran his fingers through his dark brown hair, ruffling it. "I'm glad Beau told us the truth yesterday. I'd be feeling a lot more skeptical about him if he hadn't. But Tanya Blair has been the bank manager for the last five years and cares very much about the town. Same with Stan Reynolds.

He was only thirty when he started his law firm here and he works really hard to be active in the community."

"You sound like you could campaign for any one of them," Molly said, fastening her seatbelt.

Sam chuckled and started the truck. "I think, no matter what, we'll be in good shape. And honestly? I'm glad Brandon is going back to being sheriff. Chris is doing a great job, but I think there's a lot of perspective that comes with age."

He pulled into the line of cars waiting to get out of the crowded lot.

"That means I'll be even smarter in a few years," Molly teased.

"I think I should be scared," Sam joked. "Want me to drop you at *The Bulletin*?"

Biting her lip, wondering if she was completely off base, Molly tapped her fingers against her leg. "Actually, can we take a trip out to the Granger farm?"

Looking over at her, Sam just stared, waiting for the reason.

"I saw Corky."

He looked around like she meant right this second. "Where?"

"Before I went inside. This might sound crazy but I think he's sleeping at the Granger farm."

"What? Why? That's quite a way from Main Street where he usually hangs out."

Molly nodded as Sam moved forward and pulled out of the lot, onto the street. "It is. Which would account for him not coming by as frequently. I saw makeshift bedding when I was looking for kittens in John's barn, and today Corky had cat hair all over his jacket."

"That would explain why there's evidence of someone being there but no actual vandalism. Maybe we should just phone John. Let him know what you think."

"Does Corky know John?"

Sam shrugged. "Everyone knows Corky."

"True. But he's so jumpy. More so since he found Skyler's body," Molly said, referring to the celebrity chef. "Even today, with me, he was wary. If John doesn't know him other than in passing, it might freak Corky out."

"Okay. So, what are you thinking?" Sam took the turn to head out of town, toward the farm.

"I texted Calli and asked her to meet us there. She's closest to him. Her and Bella. I'm thinking that if she's there, he'll spook less easily."

Sam reached over the console and took her hand. "If he is staying there, I'm not sure how John is going to feel about that."

"I know. Which is why I'm hoping Calli can convince him to go to the shelter."

Part of her hoped—expected, even—to see Corky walking the long stretch of road that they took to the farm. But in all likelihood, if she was right about her hunch, he wouldn't take the narrow, two-lane street. He'd weave in and out of the paths, forests, and farms. The walk would be shorter that way.

Calli was talking to John when they pulled up to the farmhouse, a gorgeous two-story home. Painted a deep forest green, it had black shutters on each window and beautiful window boxes on the lower ones. Flowers bloomed brightly from each of the three boxes. On the porch, a white swing swayed in the breeze.

John, looking even taller with the addition of a cowboy hat today, was nodding at whatever Calli was saying. She was dressed in her usual jeans and a t-shirt, her hair up in a messy bun. She carried a paper bag that Molly suspected was full of food.

They got out of the car and joined the other two.

"Molly, Sam. Calli here tells me you think I've got a stowaway," John said. He actually tipped his hat their way, making Molly smile.

Sam hooked his thumb in Molly's direction. "Molly ran into Corky today."

Calli's smile slipped. "How did he look?"

"Nervous. A little thin. But happy. And covered in cat hair," Molly said.

"If he's staying in that particular barn, it's dangerous. It's basically our storage unit that I haven't gotten around to organizing. Only time I'm in there is to feed the cats and toss more stuff in."

"Which would make it easy for him to stay under the radar," Sam said.

"Let's go check it out." John led the way to the barn. When they neared it, the puppies spotted them and came barrelling forward. They must have been playing somewhere, but now that they'd spotted people, their huge paws couldn't carry them fast enough. All of them stopped to pay some attention and Molly couldn't hold back the laughter when one of them nibbled on her hair.

"You sure you don't want one?" John asked.

She smiled up at him from her crouch. "We talked about it, but we just don't have the room."

"I want one but we spend so much time at the restaurant," Calli said, rubbing the smallest one's belly with one hand and holding the bag of food up with the other.

They continued on their way. The farm was quite expansive, and walking from the main house took them a few minutes. They stopped outside of it and hesitated, as if by silent agreement.

"We don't want to scare him," Calli said.

"He might not even be here yet," Sam said.

"But if he's been staying here, I should be able to tell now that you've said something," John added.

The door was open a crack. John pulled it open further, slowly, the door bumping over the gravel underneath. Cats immediately moved around, meowing and approaching them.

"This here is one of the mamas," John said, picking up a brown and orange cat who curled around his legs.

"She's gorgeous," Calli said. "Maybe Dean and I should get a kitten."

John's laugh filled the dimly lit barn. "I happen to have a few if you're serious."

Probably smelling the food, three kittens wandered to Calli and rubbed themselves against her jeans. "Hello, you cute little things."

Sam was smiling when he looked over at Molly. She pointed to the far corner. Calli noticed and gave a curt nod, starting in that direction.

"Careful you don't trip," John said quietly.

She nodded again, watching her step as she moved around saddles, old car parts, the front of a tractor, and several other obstacles. Much like Molly had the day she'd been here. Several cats followed her, some of them jumping up on various things, almost like they wanted to lead the way.

It was hard to see her once she got deeper into the barn, but they all heard the slight gasp.

It was followed by her voice. "Hi, Corky. How you doing? I brought you some food."

Chapter Twenty-Three

Molly waited while everyone gathered around the layout table. They had a lot to get done before Thursday's edition ran. With any luck, they'd be printing the tribute to Magnolia along with the truth about who killed her. Alan came out of his office, joining her, Gavin, Jill, Hannah, and Elizabeth.

His salt and pepper hair was in need of a trim and looked like he'd been running his hands through it, which he did when he was stressed. There was a lot going on and Alan took reporting the news seriously. It was part of why he'd hired her at *The Bulletin*. He'd wanted to return to accurate, factual stories that mattered to the readers. They'd gotten away from that in recent years but they were on their way back. And then some.

Alan nodded, meeting her curious gaze. "She was not impressed but she'll be here this afternoon."

"Who will?" Elizabeth asked, looking up from her notebook.

"A source," Molly said, not ready to fill the others in.

"I can't wait any longer to hear about Corky. Everyone's here, please tell us," Jill said.

They knew that she, Calli, and Sam had gone out to the farm and found him yesterday. They'd been there for hours and Molly had texted Jill updates.

"Is he okay? Did he go to the shelter?" Alan asked.

Molly sat on one of the stools like the others. Gavin raised his hand, his dark eyes apologetic. "Sorry, but who is Corky?"

Hannah filled him in, doing an excellent job summing it up briefly and including valuable facts about the homeless situation.

Molly beamed. "Hannah, you are going to make such a good reporter."

Alan chuckled. "I second that. Well done, sweetheart. Excellent summary," Alan said to his niece.

Hannah blushed under the praise. She was such a sweet and talented girl. They'd miss her when she went off to college in September.

"Calli found him curled up in the corner?" Jill prompted.

Molly nodded. "He was sort of hiding and cowering. He kept saying no one comes in there during the day. He wouldn't take the food from Calli at first but she kept telling him he wasn't in trouble. I think he was on his way to believing her when we approached. It might have been too much all at once."

"John is a large and imposing man," Elizabeth said. "Sweet as anything, but I'd be nervous in his presence if I didn't know him and I was squatting in his barn."

"What'd Corky do?" Alan took a seat on a stool across from Molly.

Her stomach cramped at the memory of seeing the fear in Corky's eyes at being caught by the farmer. "He looked so sad and scared. John took off his hat and introduced himself. His voice was so soft. He was like a gentle giant. Corky kept apologizing, looking around like he wanted to escape. A few of the kittens came over and started nuzzling him and it distracted him. None of us really had a plan but John asked him if he'd been taking care of the kittens."

"Aww. That's why he told you the kittens love him," Jill said.

Molly nodded, glancing at the time on her phone. They needed to get going on the layout, but everyone needed to hear the story. They were going to print it in the paper. Happy endings didn't happen nearly enough in real life.

"Yup. Corky kept going back and forth saying that they loved him, he was sorry, and he likes the kittens. They started sniffing around the bag and Calli opened it. The more cats that came around, the more he relaxed. Honestly, none of us knew John was going to offer him a job and a place to live. I don't even know if John knew."

"You're kidding," Elizabeth said with a dreamy sigh. Her blondish gray hair was done up in a pretty bun and she leaned forward, resting her chin on both hands.

"Nope. He asked Corky if he could keep looking after the cats and told him that if he did, he could stay in the barn. Corky, of course, said no, he'd leave, he was sorry for being there. John said no one would take care of the cats if he left. Then he told Corky he'd been meaning to clean up the barn so the cats could move around and he sure could use some help."

"He made him feel needed," Gavin said.

Molly nodded, unable to swallow down the emotion she still felt. She sniffled. "He did. Corky said he could help. John asked if he wanted to sleep in the stable hand's house. They don't use it anymore because none of their workers live on site. It's run down because it hasn't been used, but functional. Has a bathroom and shower. A kitchen. Corky said he wanted to stay with the cats. John told him he could stay with the cats and help with the barn. In return, he'd make sure he had three meals a day and he could clean up in the other house any time he wanted."

"Oh my goodness," Hannah said, wiping a few tears. "That's so awesome. That makes me so happy. Do you think he'll stay?"

Molly shrugged. "I hope so. Calli and Dean are going to provide meals, too. It's a small step but a big one."

"Agreed. That's one hell of a happy ending to print," Alan said.

"It is. It'll add something special to this week's paper for sure." Molly stood up and went to the white board where she'd listed this week's stories and items for the paper.

"Okay. Onto other things. We can work together on Corky's story, but Elizabeth—I was thinking you'd take the lead?"

"I'd love to," Elizabeth said.

"Molly?" Hannah asked, stealing a glance at her uncle before meeting Molly's gaze.

"What's up?"

"I, uh, well, with Corky having a happy ending, maybe it'd be a great sideline to mention that so has Naomi. The people of our community are stepping up in small ways, but they matter. It's only two people, but by opening their hearts and their minds, the community has helped them go from homeless to contributing citizens. Could I interview Naomi? I'm doing an art class at Sarah's tonight anyway."

Molly took a deep breath and when she let it out, her body shuddered. "Hannah, when you are an award-winning journalist known worldwide for not only your insight but your heart, will you please come back and visit?"

They all laughed and Alan got up, going around the table to give Hannah a hug. "She'd better."

They moved through the rest of the stories, discussing the layout and the regular editorials. The pictures of the finalists for the Spring Flower Barrel Challenge, who had been chosen online, would run this week. It would be quite the eclectic mix.

"Everyone good on what needs to be done?" Molly asked, putting the cap on her whiteboard marker.

"You got it, boss," Jill said, pushing her stool back. Hannah and Gavin went to their own workstations and Elizabeth headed toward the kitchen.

Jill walked over to Molly, eyeing her suspiciously. "What are you up to?"

Molly grinned. "I have someone coming in to see me. Well, Alan, really."

Jill looked back and forth between Molly and Alan.

"What's going on?" Jill asked, her voice low enough not to be overheard by the others.

Alan shook his head. When Molly had asked him to do her this favor, she'd had to give him the basic details.

"What do you think she's doing? She's investigating a murder."

Jill rubbed her hands together. "Who is coming in?"

"Vivien Sweet. I told her that her credit card was declined and she needed to come in and make the payment to run the ad," Alan said, wincing.

"Crass, I know. I'm sorry," Molly said to him. "But it's necessary. I promise. She's lying about something and I'm going to find out, once and for all, what it is."

Chapter Twenty-Four

Vivien Sweet might not have had the reputation for publicly dressing down those around her but she knew how to play the game. By the time she arrived, her brother in tow, she was over an hour and a half late. The others had gone home but Alan stuck around.

Removing her oversized sunglasses as she entered, Jeffrey holding the door for her, her mouth was set in a brightly painted flat line.

Alan looked up from where he was seated at Elizabeth's desk. "You must be Ms. Sweet."

He stood and came around the table and her lips curved slightly upward. "Vivien. And this is my brother, Jeffrey."

"Alan Benedict, and I believe you know Molly Owens, our editor," Alan said as Molly joined them.

"We do. Molly. Nice to see you. We'd really like to clear this up quickly. I'm not quite sure why it was declined. I assure you we have more than enough money."

Jeffrey snickered. "Especially now."

Both Alan and Molly's mouths dropped open. Vivien shot her brother a hard look. The smile slipped from his face. "Let's just clear this up, shall we? How much do we owe for the full page?"

"Alan will address that with you, but Vivien, would you mind following me to my office. I have a few follow-up questions for you." Molly gestured toward her office on the other side of the room.

Vivien's tanned shoulders, covered by the straps of a silk tank top, stiffened. "I don't see why. I'm not giving interviews. I don't want to talk about my mother anymore. My brother and I are grieving. We'd just like to pay this and leave."

Molly glanced at Alan but pressed forward. *This could end badly.* "It's about Tiffany."

"The director?" Jeffrey asked.

Molly wasn't looking at him when he spoke. Instead, she watched the way Vivien's eyes widened just a fraction and her fingers, still free of nail polish, gripped her purse strap.

"Clear up the bill, Jeffrey. We'll just be a moment." She walked past Molly and into her office.

Now or never. Molly closed the door to her office and, instead of sitting behind her desk, chose to press the advantage of close proximity. Vivien didn't make eye contact when Molly sat in the chair beside her. Their knees almost touched but Vivien remained stiff and aloof.

"You said you arrived the night after your mother's death," Molly said, giving the woman a chance to correct herself.

Vivien's eyes flicked up and then beyond Molly. "So?"

"So, that's not true."

The woman's crystal blue gaze met Molly's. She wouldn't have been surprised to feel smoke come out of her head just from the heat of that glare. "Excuse me?"

Molly folded her hands together and leaned forward. "We don't have a lot of time. An innocent man has been accused of murder, and my guess is once the funeral is said and done, you and your brother will not be sticking around."

Vivien leaned back, taking her time crossing one leg over the other. She wore dark navy dress pants that rode high on her waist, her pale pink tank top tucked in.

"Why would we? My mother wanted to live here. We never did. And Judd Brown was arrested because he was guilty." A mean smile tipped her painted lips upward. "Unless the true killer is the only other person who arrived at the theater far earlier than necessary."

Aaand you just showed your hand. "I wasn't really that early, but it begs an interesting question. How do you know I was even supposed to go to the theater?"

Vivien fiddled with her purse. "I...it was in the police statement that you were there. Why *were* you there?"

Molly smiled. "To meet your mother and ask for an interview. Tiffany told me it was a good time. You know Tiffany, don't you?"

Watching the woman roll her eyes, Molly bit back a grin. "The director?" she prodded.

"Of course, I know her. I hired her," Vivien snapped, uncrossing her leg and shifting in her seat.

"You did. You argued with her before your mother's death. You lied about having been at the theater and you don't need to deny that. I already know it's true. You also lied about your arrival. Now, I don't much care when you got into town or what your relationship with Tiffany is, but what I do care about is someone getting blamed for something they didn't do. It wasn't Judd. And I can't help thinking that if, God forbid, something ever happened to my mother, I'd want the real killer brought to justice." Molly paused, taking a breath. "Unless, of course, I had a hand in her death."

Whether she'd ever done any acting, Molly didn't know, but in her personal opinion, Vivien's gasp of shock was completely genuine.

Her expression went from surprise to outrage and she shot up from her seat, pacing behind the chair. "You think I *killed* my own mother? What are you, a lunatic?"

Molly worked to keep her voice very even as she stood up and leaned against her desk. "I'm not. I'm just an editor at a small-town newspaper who knows that all of your dots aren't lining up. And if someone doesn't follow this, Judd Brown could go away for a very long time."

"I didn't kill my mother. If you print that, or anything like that, I'll have so many lawyers all over you, you won't be able to take a breath," she said, pointing at Molly.

"And you'd be able to afford that, wouldn't you? As the primary beneficiary for your mother's estate."

Vivien stopped pacing and gave Molly a glare that could have chilled the sun. "How do you know that?"

"My job is to find out things," Molly said, her voice free of emotion. Not entirely true, but she was finding out something right now—Vivien was definitely hiding things.

"Your job is to report the truth," Vivien spat.

Molly stood straight and closed the distance between them. "You're right. Why don't you give it to me? Where were you when your mother was killed? What did you fight with Tiffany about?"

Vivien leaned into Molly's space, so close she could practically taste the expensive perfume. "You are nothing but a small-town busybody. Tiffany is my employee and I argued with her about her *job*. I showed up a few days early to try to support my mother, which, like this, was a waste of my time."

She pushed past Molly and yanked open the door. "Jeffrey? Let's go."

Jeffrey followed behind his sister, glancing at Molly but not saying a word. When they left, Alan walked across the room to Molly.

"How'd that go?" He folded his arms over his chest.

"Not great. She's still hiding something but I don't think she killed her mom."

"Who does that leave?" Alan met her gaze.

"Jeffrey, though I have my doubts. But at the moment, I'm almost certain that it was Tiffany. There's something going on between those two women." Molly sighed and started moving around the office, tidying up, her mind swirling in circles.

"What are you thinking?" Alan walked to the front door and locked it.

Glancing up, she said the first thing that came to her mind. "I need to find evidence that links Tiffany and Vivien. Texts, emails, anything. What if Tiffany killed Magnolia *for* Vivien for whatever reason but Vivien has no idea?"

Walking slowly toward her, Alan gave her a look that reminded Molly of her dad. "Then that means Tiffany is a very dangerous woman and you should be careful."

Chapter Twenty-Five

Molly was grateful that Jill had the rehearsal schedule. She was able to show up at the theater the next morning before Tiffany, who, according to Cora, was keeping Magnolia's original schedule. Tomorrow was Thursday and though Chris certainly hadn't put a deadline on her, she felt a sense of urgency to solve the mystery before Jeffrey and Vivien left town. For all she knew, Tiffany would quickly follow once the play ran through its two-week production schedule.

The auditorium was sort of creepy without the actors in it. The lights were on, thankfully, but every step Molly took on the stage creaked. Her fingers gripped the two lattes she carried and she was grateful for their warmth. She didn't step on the painted path that resembled the yellow brick road but she did follow alongside it to where it met the backdrop and continued on and upward, giving it a 3-D effect.

When she looked up at the house, her pulse scrambled. It hung still and quiet, like it hadn't been sitting atop a person. On opening night, they'd drop it again and the scene she'd stumbled on with Judd and Magnolia would be reproduced in art. Molly shuddered.

The door to the auditorium opened. Molly watched Tiffany, who stared down at her phone, walk down the aisle. She started for the stairs so they could be on even ground but the creak gave her away.

Tiffany looked up. "What are you doing here?" Her voice was angry and quite loud, echoing in the space.

Molly descended the stairs and stopped in front of Tiffany in the first row of seats. Tiffany yanked off her purse and shoved her phone in it, then unzipped the hoodie she was wearing with quick, sharp movements, tossing it onto a closed seat on top of her purse.

Molly's heart rate sped up. Perfect opportunity. She didn't have anything actually planned other than showing up and trying to get something close to the truth, but an idea popped into her head and she knew there wouldn't be another opportunity like this one.

"I wanted to talk to you," Molly said, still holding the drinks.

"And Vivien. Are you trying to get me fired?"

"No. I'm just trying to figure out who really killed Magnolia."

Tiffany crossed her arms under her breasts and jutted out one hip. There was a bland expression on her face, but Molly caught the quiver of her lips.

"You're just a nosy reporter. Find something else to do. If you come here again before opening night or bother me or any of my cast and crew, I'll have you banned until I leave."

Molly stepped forward just a bit. "I don't want that. But Vivien lied about several things. Judd didn't kill Magnolia. I think you know that. If Vivien did—"

Tiffany threw her hands up in the air. "Oh my God. You're a conspiracy theorist. She did *not* kill her mother. If you don't back off, Molly, you're going to regret it."

"Is that a threat?"

Tiffany closed her eyes briefly and when she opened them, they pleaded with Molly. "No. It's a warning. Back off. Let this lie. The evidence against Judd is circumstantial. He'll walk away unscathed. If you don't stop pushing this, you won't."

Molly wasn't sure what she expected but it was not the fear that clearly shone in Tiffany's eyes. Those weren't the eyes of a killer. She was petrified.

"If not you, who? Who will hurt me?" Molly came a little closer.

"I'm telling you to stop. If you stop, he won't hurt you. Just let it go. Please."

Molly's heart hitched. "He? Jeffrey?"

Tiffany's eyes widened. "What about him?"

"Is he who you're scared of? Did he hurt Magnolia?"

With a screech like groan, Tiffany reached up and locked her fingers in her hair, pushing it back from her face. "Jeffrey wouldn't hurt something if he had a ten-step list of how to go about it. Stop, Molly. Or you'll have no one to blame but yourself for the consequences."

Confusion crowded her thoughts. Going with her impromptu plan, she extended her hand, offering the lukewarm coffee. "I'm sorry I upset you. Here, this is for you."

Tiffany eyed her suspiciously and just when she reached for it, Molly let it slip from her grasp, eliciting a cry from Tiffany. Immediately, Molly crouched and began apologizing.

"I'm sorry, I'm such a klutz. Do you have a rag? Is there a janitor? I'm so sorry, Tiffany."

The director huffed out an impatient sigh. "It's okay. Just…just give me a minute. I'll go see if I can find some paper towels backstage."

Tiffany took the stairs to the right and disappeared behind the curtain. Molly set the other coffee down and wasted zero seconds moving Tiffany's sweater and unzipping the woman's purse.

The "he" didn't make sense, but if Molly could prove that Tiffany had a relationship with Vivien, that they'd said something incriminating, maybe she could take that to Chris. With trembling hands, Molly dug around in the black, name-brand purse, looking for the phone she'd watched Tiffany put inside. She saw it at the bottom of the purse, but when she moved the plastic bag above it, she caught sight of what was inside.

Pulling her own phone out of her pocket, she held up the bag full of over-the-counter sedatives and snapped a picture, her heart beating so loud in her ears she couldn't even hear her own breathing. She set the bag back inside and then pulled out the phone. It was locked. Why hadn't she thought of that? Of course it was locked. Tiffany's footsteps sounded over the ragged thump of her heart. Molly shoved the phone back in, zipped up the purse and pulled the sweater over it just as Tiffany pushed through the curtain, paper towels in hand.

With shaky hands, Molly accepted the paper towel Tiffany offered and both of them crouched to sop up the liquid. Molly's hand moved back and forth in jerky movements.

"Careful, or you'll knock yours over, too," Tiffany said, pressing the towel into the spill.

Molly's laugh was too loud. "Ha. Yeah. Well, I think you get that one. I'll grab one on the way home. I'm really sorry for bugging you. I just want to help Judd."

Tiffany met her gaze and both of them stopped cleaning. "I get that. But you're in over your head here. Let it go, Molly."

Molly nodded, swallowing around the knot lodged in her throat.

* * * *

Molly locked the doors of her Jeep and looked around, like someone might have followed her. She texted Chris the picture of the sedatives and then dialed his number.

"Beatty," he answered.

"It's Molly."

"That's what the call display said too, so it must be true," he replied.

She didn't have it in her to laugh. "I texted you a picture. Did you get it?"

"Uh, no. You called and I answered. Feeling needy today?"

"Chris, what kind of sedatives were found in Magnolia's body?"

He must have realized it wasn't a friendly call. "What's going on?" His voice was now full-on cop.

"Do you see the picture?"

She heard nothing for a moment and knew he was checking. She heard him swear before he came back on the line. "Where did you find those?"

"In Tiffany's purse."

"Where are you?"

"Are they the same pills?"

"They're a generic over-the-counter pill, Molly. Where are you?"

"Are they the same?"

"Dammit, Molly. Where are you?"

She gripped the steering wheel. "I'm at the theater. Are they the same?"

"Yes," Chris muttered. "I need to get a warrant. Listen to me, Molly—and I mean it, actually *listen*—you did good, but I want you to get away from the theater and stay away from it. Stay away from Tiffany and everyone else involved with the play. You're done."

He hung up before she could tell him about Tiffany's warning.

Chapter Twenty-Six

Molly was on edge for the rest of the day. If she went home, she'd be restless and bored. Pushing through the day, trying not to reveal how shaken she was at being right, at the idea that Tiffany had murdered her boss and somehow framed Judd, she kept reading lines over and over again.

Sam called halfway through the day to say hello. When he asked about grabbing something to eat, she said she had to finish up a few things. If she saw him while she was still on edge, she wouldn't be able to keep the fear out of her voice when she told him everything. No, she'd collect herself, get her emotions under control, hope Chris got the warrant reasonably quick, and tell Sam everything after work.

"Why don't I go grab Tigger and we'll walk over to *The Bulletin* after I'm done here? You can leave your Jeep there and we'll walk down to the water?"

"That sounds good," she said, her voice sounding distant in her own head.

"You okay?"

Breathing through her nose, she nodded, even though he couldn't see her. "I am. I miss you. I'll be done around six."

"Sounds good. Love you."

"I love you, too."

When she hung up, she did her best to stay in the moment. By five o'clock, she was feeling less restless. She wished Chris would phone her back or text and let her know if he had a warrant. *You're done.* Right. She got that, but it didn't mean she didn't want to know how things wrapped up.

Elizabeth and Jill waved goodbye as they headed out together. Alan would take care of running off the newspapers and distributing them to vendors. As a trade-off for his long Wednesday hours, he typically took Thursdays off.

Tomorrow, they'd start working on the next edition. The news never stopped. Sometimes, Molly found that strange. By the time people opened their newspapers, a new truth would have come to light. They'd have to update the website and social media if Chris had any news. Alone in the news office, with Alan downstairs and the others gone, Molly's restlessness came back.

She picked up her phone and dialed Sam. He picked up on the first ring. "Hey. I just got home. Tigger approves of our evening plans."

Molly laughed, less tension crowding her chest. "I'm actually finished here so if you give me ten minutes, I'll be home and we can just walk to the beach from there?"

"Okay. That sounds good. You want to try that new fish and chip shop on the pier? They have outdoor seating so Tigger will be fine."

"That sounds perfect," Molly said, her stomach grumbling. She grabbed her bag and the sweater she'd pulled on this morning, and headed for the back of the building.

"You sound tired," Sam said.

Molly checked the coffee maker to make sure it was off and paused at the countertop. "Long day. I'll tell you all about it."

"Okay. See you in a few."

She hung up, slipping her phone in her back pocket. Taking an extra minute to put a few mugs in the dishwasher and turn it on, she gave a final glance around the room. Satisfied with the state of the small kitchen that served as a break room, she walked to the back door.

Outside, the sun shone brightly and it warmed Molly's chilled skin. *Should have dug my keys out,* she thought as she approached her Jeep. Unzipping her bag, her fingers had just closed around the cool metal when she heard something behind her. Before she could turn all the way around, something struck her head. Hard. A streak of pain whipped through her head, making her cry out. She glimpsed a flash of black in the seconds before she fell to the ground. Her eyelids grew heavy as she crumpled to the pavement. A small whimper left her mouth when something hard connected with her ribs, making them feel like they'd cracked into splintered pieces. After that, she felt nothing.

* * * *

Molly woke in the back of a police cruiser, her mouth dry and her head pounding. It took effort to open her eyelids and make sense of what was happening.

"Molly?" Sam's voice pierced through the fog.

It took a minute for him to come all the way into focus.

"Is she awake?"

Who was that? Chris? Why was she in a cop car?

"Sam," she whispered. Her throat felt like a desert.

"I'm here. Just rest. We're almost at the hospital," Sam said, his face close.

She realized that she was lying across his lap—sitting in it, really. His arms were a vice around her, which was probably good since she didn't think she was wearing a seatbelt. Trying to pull in a breath, she winced at the sharp slice of pain.

"Keep her awake, Sam. If she's awake, keep talking to her," Chris said.

He was driving. Why was he driving?

"What hurts?" Sam asked, noticing her pain.

"Everything." The word stuck in her throat. "But mostly my ribs."

Chris zipped into the hospital parking lot, parking in front of the emergency room doors. He told them to stay there and disappeared. What seemed like seconds later, the back door opened and two doctors, or nurses, or orderlies—Molly wasn't entirely sure—appeared.

The next several moments were painful and somewhat embarrassing. Molly didn't feel like she could support her own weight for any length of time, but no one was allowing her to even try. She was pushed into a wheelchair, despite Sam's insistence that he could carry her, past the nurse's station and into the back of the hospital.

"A doctor will be right with her, Sheriff," a man said. He wore dark green scrubs and had held her gently while he helped her into the wheelchair. Smiling at Molly, he approached slowly. "Let's take your blood pressure while we wait, okay?"

Sam held her hand while the guy checked and Chris paced in front of the cordoned off area. She could hear monitors and voices, beeps and murmurs. Pressure built behind her eyes and her head felt heavy.

"Can she lie down?" Sam barked, his tone unusually sharp.

"Sure she can," a woman entering the room in a white jacket with a stethoscope around her neck replied.

"Sheriff," the woman greeted.

"Dr. Remy."

The doctor waited for Sam and the blood pressure guy—Molly didn't even try to read his name tag because her eyes wanted to cross or shut—to help her onto the bed. She tried to downplay the wincing but pain jolted through her.

"Hi, Molly. I'm Ramona Remy. Do you know where you are?" She smiled at Molly kindly. She had light brown hair cut just below her chin and brown eyes. She didn't look familiar, but Molly wasn't sure now was the best time to wonder.

"Hospital or a really bad play."

Ramona's grin stretched. "You have a sense of humor. Do you remember what happened?"

Sam stayed close to her side while Molly thought about it. When she didn't answer right away, he spoke. "When I found her, she was on the cement, passed out and curled into a little ball."

"Hmm. Do you remember how you got that way?" Dr. Remy checked Molly's eyes, which hurt on the left side where she was pretty sure she'd been hit.

"Something hit me from behind. I didn't see what or who. And I think I got kicked in the ribs. They hurt. A lot."

"Okay. Let's take a look. Sheriff, why don't you go get some water for your friend. She sounds a little parched. You okay if Sam stays while I examine you?"

"I'm not leaving," Sam said.

Molly managed to smile as Sam helped her shift to lie down. "It's fine."

She shut the curtain before coming back and lifting Molly's shirt slowly. Molly wanted to see, but she couldn't lift her neck without it hurting her ribs. It must not have looked great though because Sam hissed and swore.

"Looks tender for sure. I'm going to finish checking you and then I'm going to send you for some x-rays and a CT scan."

The doctor did just that and even though it seemed to take hours of her life, Molly didn't really mind because through it all she could close her eyes on and off and rest. She was tired and wanted nothing more than to go home. Unfortunately, she didn't get to do that until hours later.

Chapter Twenty-Seven

Sam hovered, but she couldn't even get mad at him because she'd do the same in his position. Chris, however, stalked like an animal about to pounce. While Molly tried to get comfortable on the couch, the two argued under their breath and she only caught bits of what they were saying.

"If you don't go easy on her, I *will* kick you out," Sam muttered, closing the fridge.

"I'm not a monster. I'm just going to talk to her." Chris grabbed the juice Sam had poured and brought it over to Molly.

Sam met her gaze, his hands fumbling with the painkillers the doctor had prescribed. "Let me know if you want me to toss him, okay?"

Molly smiled. Laughing would hurt. Chris passed her the juice. "You said at the hospital that Tiffany told you something bad would happen. You don't think you could have mentioned that to me when we spoke?"

Accepting the juice, she took a sip, the orange citrus coating her incredibly dry mouth.

"Chris," Sam snapped.

"I'm *asking*," Chris said.

"I would have if you hadn't hung up on me. I was coming home to tell Sam everything and then I figured you'd be the next call."

Sam brought her two pills but she only took one. He scowled, so she conceded and took both.

"Next time, how about I'm your *first* call," Chris said, sitting on the coffee table.

"I don't think so," Sam said, pulling the armchair closer to the couch and sitting in it.

"I'm the cop, Sam. She doesn't need you charging to the rescue."

"She wouldn't have needed rescuing if you hadn't asked her to do your job," Sam said, taking the juice so Molly didn't have to stretch.

Chris's face paled.

"Sam," Molly whispered. "It's not his fault."

"You know I would never want her to get hurt. You *know* that," Chris said. He sounded distraught at the idea that they might not.

"We know that. It's no one's fault. Well, other than whoever did this."

"We don't have a warrant yet but we should by the end of business hours tomorrow. The judge in the next county was backed up so we're pushing as quick as we can," Chris said. "You can't remember anything?"

Molly closed her eyes a minute and tried to remember the seconds before. They were blurry. When she opened her eyes, both Sam and Chris were staring at her intently. "I can't. I'm sorry. I heard a sound but I didn't see anything or anyone."

"I'm just glad you're okay. Minus some bruised ribs, some scrapes and a black eye." Sam took her hand and squeezed it.

"I'm sorry I scared you."

"You're lucky you don't have a concussion. I'm not going to question Tiffany until I have the warrant. I don't want to spook her and have her run off," Chris said.

"You know she's behind this," Sam said, standing up. He walked over to the fireplace and flicked the switch. Summer might have been on the way but Molly felt chilled all the way through her skin.

"I do. She's definitely involved."

"She's scared, Chris. I don't know who she's scared of, but something bigger is going on here. She tried to warn me."

Chris sighed. "You think it's Jeffrey?"

Molly shook her head and then regretted it. "I don't. I don't know who it is. I'm positive that there's something between Vivien and Tiffany but I don't know what. But when she told me I'd regret it, she said *he'd* hurt me."

"We're going to figure it out, Molly. I promise. And by we, I mean me and my department. All you need to do is rest," Chris said, his tone bordering on lecturing.

"Maybe I should call her, tell her to talk to you. If you could make her feel safe, like whoever she's working with can't hurt her, maybe she'll open up."

Sam groaned. "You can't contact her, Molly. You just got out of the hospital. Can you let this go and let Chris do his job?"

Molly nodded, fatigue making it hard to argue any of their points. Their voices drifted further away as Molly's body slipped down on the couch.

Her head felt blissful against the cushions. She'd return to the conversation soon. She just needed a few minutes to rest and get her thoughts together. Then she'd tell Chris again that instead of just investigating Tiffany, she had a feeling he needed to protect her as well.

* * * *

Molly spent the entire next day under Sam's watchful eye. She loved that he cared so much for her, but she was going stir-crazy by mid-afternoon. Though her ribs ached, her head felt better.

"At least we know I can't pull off a black eye," she said, coming out of the bathroom where she'd just finished showering. It hurt too much to have her hair up in a wrap, so she just wrung it out and put a towel over her shoulders.

"Not funny," Sam said, putting his arm around her.

"Did you wait outside the bathroom? Are you trying to replace Tigger?" Sam had asked his mom to come down and get their pup while Molly had been at the hospital. She'd insisted on keeping him for a few days so he didn't accidentally jump up and startle Molly.

They walked toward the couch. "I wanted to be there in case you felt dizzy."

"I'm okay, Sam." Patting his hand, she brought it to her mouth and kissed it. "Promise."

"I need to go into the shop tomorrow morning but I'll take the afternoon off," Sam said, helping her ease into a sitting position on their couch without jolting her ribs.

"That's silly. I'm going to work tomorrow."

Sam scowled as he settled beside her, picking up the remote. "Damn it, Molly. You have bruised ribs and a black eye. How about you stay home for two days? Alan said to take a week."

"That's ridiculous. I'm fine to sit at my desk. Or at least pick my stuff up so I can work from home."

"Jill can bring you your stuff," Sam countered, settling on a home renovation show. He tossed the remote beside him.

"And I can go get it just as easily without interrupting anyone else's life."

Sam's head turned in her direction. "Is that what you think? That you being hurt is an interruption?"

Molly was surprised by the sharpness of his tone. "No. But, I don't need people waiting on me. I feel bad enough you have to."

Shifting on the cushion, he angled his body toward her and took her hand. "Do you understand how relationships work? I don't just mean ours. We're in love and committed and our promise to each other is to be there for each other no matter what. At least, that's how I feel."

Reaching out, she cupped his stubbled jaw. "I feel that way, too, Sam. You know I do. I just hate when you worry."

His hand covered hers on his cheek and he leaned into it. "It's not just me, though, Molly. My mom, Brandon, Chris, Sarah, Jill, Alan, everyone you *know* is worried about you. They *love* you. Just like you'd worry for them or maybe cater to them a bit, they want to help, they want to have your back. If you care about people, you have to let them all the way in, Molly. You're not alone. You have me. My family. Our friends. Pretending that you don't need them is an insult to them."

Tears stung her eyes and he sighed, leaning forward to kiss her softly. "I'm not trying to upset you. You always think you have to be this strong, *I-can-do-it-myself* woman. But sometimes you can show the greatest strength by asking for help."

She nodded, tugging on his hand lightly to pull him close again. After several short, sweet kisses, she smiled at him. "You can ask Jill to bring me my stuff. But stay at work until lunchtime tomorrow."

"Molly."

"That way you can bring me something from Calli's on your way."

Sam grinned. "You got it."

Chapter Twenty-Eight

Sam was gone before Molly woke up the next morning. Though she moved slowly, she managed to dress in yoga pants and a T-shirt, and put on a pair of socks without crying out in pain. When she shuffled into the kitchen, stiff and sore, coffee was waiting. He was such a good guy. She sent a quick text to thank him. Missing Tigger, she debated going up to the house and grabbing him, but decided his exuberance might be too much for her ribs.

Pouring a cup of coffee, she took it to the back deck, liking the idea that this could be their new routine all summer. Sam had found a tall plant stand in his mom's shed that they were using for a table between their two chairs. It was a little low-budget, but once the deck was finished and stained, they'd pick something nice together.

Molly put the coffee down and eased her way into the chair. Her ribs protested and a small groan left her lips. As she settled, she gritted her teeth and tried to breathe slowly. If it hurt this much to have bruised ribs, she couldn't even imagine the pain people felt when they were broken.

Her phone buzzed before she could take a drink.

Jill: You up and moving around?

Molly: I am. Are you at the paper?

Jill: Yes. Need anything other than your laptop? Which you don't actually need because you could rest instead of work.

Molly: I have a couple notebooks in the top right drawer of my desk. Can you bring those with you, too?

Jill: Yup. Way to ignore the above statement.

Molly: I prefer the word evade.

Jill: That is a good one. Muffins from Bella's?

Molly: A 1000 times yes.

Jill: LOL See you soon.

Molly set her phone down and focused on drinking her coffee, willing her brain to stay away from anything to do with Magnolia. Chris would have the warrant today. And Tiffany would likely be arrested. Unless whoever hurt Molly got to her first.

Her phone buzzed again.

Katherine: Need anything? I'm headed out for a couple of hours. Sam took Tigger to work with him.

Molly grinned.

Molly: I'm okay. Thank you.

Katherine: You're feeling all right?

Molly: Better today. Don't worry.

Katherine: Nice try. I'll stop by later.

Since she was holding her phone anyway, she decided it was fine to check *The Bulletin*'s social media. Everything looked great but she couldn't stop thinking about how, by the next edition, Judd could be cleared.

Trying to think about something else, she typed in patio sets and spent some time browsing through ones she thought Sam might like. That rabbit hole didn't pull her attention all the way, but it kept her busy until Jill texted and said she was there.

When she opened the door, her mouth watered just from looking at the logo on the white paper take-out bag.

Molly reached out. "You're the best."

Jill smiled. "That's what they all say."

Heading into the house, Jill unloaded the laptop on Molly's couch. "Notebooks are in the side pocket."

Molly bit down on her lip, holding back the words that wanted to spill out as she set muffins on a plate, sliding one across the counter when Jill sat on the barstool.

Jill let out a heavy sigh. "What's wrong?"

Molly's gaze flew to her friend's. She knew her well. "I can't stop thinking about Tiffany."

Jill's eyes widened and she lowered her chin. "The murderer?"

Breaking off a piece of muffin, Molly ate it before replying. "I don't think she is. She's involved. Obviously. But, Jill. You should have seen the terror in her eyes."

Jaw tense, Jill flattened her hands on the countertop. "She should be scared, Molly. Either she killed Magnolia and is about to get caught or she's working with someone who did and *is about to get caught*."

Nodding, Molly tried to quiet the unease in her gut. "I need a favor."

Jill groaned, long and loud. "You're going to make Sam hate me, aren't you?"

"He could never hate you," Molly said, guilt tickling at the base of her spine.

"Until I willingly collude with his answers-obsessed girlfriend and assist her in her latest dangerous plan while she should be resting."

Molly grabbed two waters from the fridge and passed one to Jill. "Latest dangerous plan? That's not fair. I don't knowingly head into risky situations."

Jill tilted her head to one side. "Really? Shall we review?"

Molly held up her hand. "No. But I'll make you a deal. I'll tell you what I'm thinking, and if you think it's too dangerous, I won't do it."

Picking up a large piece of muffin top, Jill narrowed her eyes. "Tell me."

"We, that's *we,* not *me,* go to the hotel and make a plea, *together,* to Tiffany to go to Chris now. Before he issues the warrant. We probably shouldn't tell her about the warrant, but I know she's scared, Jill. If she knows Chris will help her—and you know he will—maybe she'll turn on whoever scares her."

Jill took her time chewing, making Molly want to squirm. "She's still part of this, Mol. She's dangerous."

"She wasn't the one who attacked me. Whoever she's working with is *more* dangerous. And if she gets arrested and the person finds out, they could be in the wind for good."

"In the wind? Who is she, Jason Bourne?"

She knew Jill was trying to make her laugh but Molly's sense of urgency wouldn't fade. Tiffany might have had something to do with Magnolia's death, but she could also be in serious trouble herself.

"I'm with you every second," Jill said.

"Done."

"We call Chris and tell him," Jill added.

Molly's shoulders sagged. "He'll stop us. I wouldn't put it past him to put me on house arrest. He'll have a deputy here before we can get to the driveway."

"I had to try."

"We'll go, make our case—maybe seeing me banged up will be enough to make her see how serious this is—and we'll leave. We'll be back before Sam brings me lunch."

Pushing the muffin away, Jill shook her head, her expression resigned. "Let's go then."

* * * *

The Sea Side Shangri-La was Britton Bay's finest, and only, hotel.
There were several motels and dozens of bed and breakfasts for tourists.
Eventually, Molly figured they'd get more hotels but for now this one
sufficed. Although it was generic, the hotel was full of amenities, boasting
four floors and several cottages around an inground pool. People who wanted
a place to stay that included room service and a workout room came here.

Jill drove Molly's Jeep because it was higher than her own car and easier
for Molly to slide into. She parked in front of the hotel. Molly realized
she hadn't been here since Skyler's death. She cringed. Maybe she did get
herself into "situations" but it was for the good of others.

Helping her out of the Jeep, Jill asked, "You sure?"

"We'll be ten minutes and then I won't involve myself any further,"
Molly said.

Jill snorted with laughter. "Right. Wish I'd recorded that."

They walked side by side into the hotel. Peak season was on its way,
but for now the lobby was quiet. Kip, whom Molly had met before, was at
the front desk. He smiled when he saw Molly and Jill.

"Morning ladies. What can I do for you?"

"We're here to see Tiffany Faye," Molly said.

Kip's smile dropped. "Is she expecting you?"

"Probably not, but we need to go over a couple of things for photos
we're taking on opening night," Jill said.

"Oh. Okay. She's in room 410."

Molly smiled at him, feeling only a mild level of guilt that it was so
easy to get what they wanted.

"Thanks, Kip. You're awesome," Jill said.

The dark-haired gangly desk manager blushed and grinned so wide
Molly was sure she could see every one of his teeth.

"No problem. Anything you need, Jill."

Molly bit her lip to hold back her smile as they walked to the elevators.
When they got in, she looked over at Jill. "Does every man in Britton Bay
have a crush on you?"

Jill scoffed. "What? Kip and I went to school together. He's a sweetie."

"I think he'd like to be *your* sweetie."

Jill rolled her eyes and stared at the round numbers lighting with each
floor. The doors slid open on the third floor. Molly saw the janitor cart
first before her eyes moved all the way up to see who was behind it.

"Oops, sorry. I'll wait—oh, Molly," Tripp, Judd's cousin, said.

Molly smiled at him. She hadn't seen him since the night at Judd's. "Hi, Tripp." A sharp stab of pain lanced through her head and she winced.

Jill immediately stepped closer and Tripp pushed the cart ahead just enough to stop the doors from closing.

"You okay?" he asked.

"Molly? Are you?" Jill wrapped an arm around Molly's shoulders.

Pressing her fingers to her temple, Molly nodded. "I'm fine. I just… my head just hurts."

"From the look of you, more than that hurts. You get in a scuffle?" Tripp asked.

Looking up at him, her vision feeling slightly off, it took her a minute to answer. Clearly, he worked here. He wore a blue T-shirt with a nametag on the right side of his chest.

"She got attacked," Jill said as Molly continued to stare.

He didn't look much like Judd. His hair was shorter and black. He wore jeans and his T-shirt had a small rip under the nametag. Judd wouldn't wear a shirt with holes in it. He had too much pride.

"Attacked? That's awful." Tripp's voice sounded far away.

"Molly, are you okay?" Jill's voice snapped through her random thoughts.

"Fine. I'm fine." Wasn't she? Maybe she was feeling worse than she thought.

Jill squeezed her shoulder again. "Sorry, but we need to get going. Are you getting on?"

"No ma'am. Company policy not to get on with guests or visitors. You have a nice day. Take care of yourself, Molly." He pulled back and the doors shut.

"You're freaking me out," Jill said, bending her knees a bit as she stood in front of Molly. "Maybe we should go."

"No. I'm fine. I don't know what happened. Just a sharp pain."

The doors slid open on the fourth floor and they quickly found room 410. Molly's heart rate had ramped up in the elevator, and she felt like it was pulsating through her entire body.

Jill knocked on the door, stealing glances at Molly, who tried to smile and pretend she didn't feel off.

The door swung open and Tiffany greeted them with a groan. "What are you doing here?" Her eyes scanned Molly. "What happened to you?"

Jill didn't give the other woman a choice. She stepped forward, dragging Molly with her and Tiffany stepped back, letting them in.

"That's what we need to know," Jill said. The door slid closed.

Tiffany was dressed in jeans and a pullover sweater that said "California" across the front. Her hair was back in a ponytail, drawing attention to how pale she looked. Whatever make-up she wore didn't hide the dark circles under her eyes.

"You two need to go. Now. Before I call security," Tiffany said.

"Actually, what we need is for you to tell us who beat Molly up," Jill countered.

They stood in the tiny hallway that led down to a bedroom. The bathroom door to the left of them was ajar, and to the right, the open closet revealed clothes spilling out of a suitcase.

"How would I know?" Tiffany crossed her arms over her chest.

"Tiffany, if you don't let us help you, whoever did this to me is going to do worse to you. You know that, right?"

"I'm not scared of that. You brought that on yourself. I warned you," Tiffany said, her eyes darting to the floor.

"I found sedatives in your purse," Molly said.

Tiffany's mouth gaped. "You went in my purse?" She stepped forward, anger contorting her features. "Who do you think you are?"

Jill stepped between them, but they all froze when the door buzzed and opened. Tripp came into the room, shutting the door behind him. Molly's heart rate tripled. Tiffany let out a panicked sound as Tripp pocketed the key card and stared at the three of them with hatred shimmering in his gaze.

Chapter Twenty-Nine

"What are you doing in here?" Jill asked, looking at Tripp.

Tiffany started to cry, pointing at Molly. "I told her to stop. This isn't my fault. Please don't hurt Vivien. She has nothing to do with any of this."

Molly's eyes flew to Tiffany and then back to Tripp. He pulled something from his back pocket. Her heart dropped to her stomach when he unfolded the knife and the metal glittered.

"Shut up. Just shut up so I can think. All of you, get into the room. Purses and phones on the dresser. Now! Sit on the bed. One of you makes a wrong move and I swear to everything holy I will make you regret it."

Shuffling with the other two, they moved to the unmade bed, all of them trying not to take their eyes off of Judd's cousin.

"Sit down. Now. Hands behind your backs." Wielding the knife in front of them as they sat leaning against each other awkwardly, he reached behind him again and pulled out something red. It took Molly a second to recognize it for what it was, but as he unwound the velvet cloth it became sickeningly clear. The other rope for the stage curtains.

"Good thing I carry everything I might need on my cart," he said with a nasty smile.

He stepped toward them, the blade of the knife coming only inches from Molly's face. Jill gripped her hand and Tiffany's sobs increased.

"Shut up. I'm going to tie you three together, but if you don't shut up, I'll make you."

Jill squeezed Molly's hand. Her ribs screamed in pain from the way she was sitting. She couldn't fight back even if he put the knife down. Tiffany was useless, and the thought of Jill getting hurt made bile rise in her throat.

They sat still while he pocketed the knife and wrapped the rope around their upper bodies, the three of them squished together, trapping their arms by their sides. The increased pressure around her made Molly wince in pain. She couldn't breathe.

"Stop crying!" Tripp shouted.

"There's no reason to do this, Tripp," Molly said. Reasoning with a madman had absolutely never worked for her in the past.

He laughed, a deep, throaty, haunting chuckle. "Wouldn't have been if you'd taken a hint and backed off."

Molly's head swam. "You *asked* me to look into who murdered Magnolia."

Tripp waved the knife in front of them and then his hand shot out, gripping a chunk of Molly's hair. His breath and the scent of his soap clogged her senses. She let out a sharp cry.

"I pointed you in the other direction. I figured you'd come up with nothing and Judd would go to prison like he damn well deserves."

With her shoulders scrunched to try to alleviate the pull of his fingers, Molly fought back tears. "For what? What did he do? He didn't kill Magnolia."

Tripp's hand dropped and he paced in front of them, the knife firmly in his grip. "Nope. He didn't. Instead, he just let her take off with all of our money." He stalked back to them, leaning down as Tiffany's whimpers quieted. "I spend my life cleaning up after other people, and even then I can't get a full-time gig doing it. I live in my cousin's dingy basement, living paycheck to paycheck. We had plans. *I* had plans. Then he cashes them in for a pretty smile from some Hollywood wench who used him? He gave her *our* money. He had no goddamn right."

Molly couldn't wade through the words, but keeping him talking felt essential. They couldn't just sit there and let him do whatever he was going to do. They had to at least try. But there was no way to communicate that to Jill.

Tripp stood straight. "This was my chance. They both got payback and now, once again, women are screwing up my life."

Molly squeezed Jill's hand in an attempt to alert her that she was going to at least try to fight back. Jill's grip turned into a death lock making it clear she was *not* on board with that plan. Panic and guilt thrashed inside of Molly's rib cage along with pain. She'd dragged Jill into this.

"We can undo this. Tiffany warned me to stay away. I should have listened. We'll walk away. You can leave town. They suspect Tiffany anyway," Molly said, which sent Tiffany into another symphony of tears.

Tripp shoved a hand into his hair, his knuckles turning white with his grip. "If. You. Don't. Stop. Crying. I'm going to go from here to your girlfriend's house and kill her. Do you understand me?"

Girlfriend? Vivien. Suddenly, it became clear whom Tiffany was protecting. She was protecting the woman she loved from what they were facing right this minute.

"Vivien?" Molly said.

"Stay away from her or I'll tell everyone it was you who killed Magnolia," Tiffany yelled, finding her voice.

Tripp lowered his hand and let out a mean laugh. "Yeah? Who you gonna tell when you're dead?"

"You can't kill all three of us and just walk out of here," Jill said, her voice utterly calm.

Tripp's breath hitched, becoming uneven. "You're right," he said quietly, crouching so he was looking at Molly and Jill. Tiffany was facing the headboard, her back to them.

Molly's feet hung off the edge of the bed, as did Jill's. If he came a little closer, maybe she could connect with his face.

Tripp smiled, freezing Molly's insides. "I can't kill all three of you and get away with it. But I could kill two of you and make it seem like Hollywood did it. She'll take the fall for you two, and Judd will take the fall for Magnolia."

A genuine, almost warm smile spread over his craggy face, as if this plan pleased him greatly.

It was literally now or never. Molly swung her foot up, barely grazing Tripp's chin and sending shots of agony spiralling from her ribs. He leaned back, rubbing his face and knocking himself off balance, landing on his butt. Jill and Molly moved at the same time, dragging Tiffany up with them so they were a tangled mess, half standing, half sitting as Tripp started to laugh.

Righting himself as they scurried all the way off the bed, all but dragging Tiffany and shoving themselves into the corner by the nightstand, he continued to laugh.

"Guess we know who I'm starting with," Tripp growled, raising the knife.

A thunderous crash sounded. Tiffany screamed as Tripp turned his head to see the commotion and men swarmed the room.

"Freeze," Chris shouted, gun drawn and pointed directly at Tripp. "Drop the knife now or I *will* shoot you."

Tripp glanced back at the three women who were wiggling the rope up and off their bodies, the fibers scratching their skin raw.

"No," Tripp said, already lowering the knife to the ground, one hand up. "This isn't what it looks like. I swear. I was just about to call the police."

When the knife touched the ground, Chris stepped forward, kicked it away, and lowered his gun. His deputies kept theirs trained on Tripp as Chris grabbed the man's arms and roughly turned him, pulling his hands behind his back.

"Is that so. And what, exactly, were you going to say?" Chris cuffed him, then patted him down.

"Tiffany killed Magnolia. She was going to kill these two but she'd convinced them I did it, so I had to tie them up until I could tell you guys the truth," Tripp said, grunting when Chris turned him around roughly.

"Wills," Chris said to one of the deputies. "Cuff Tiffany as well and read her her rights." He gestured to another deputy. "José, get Molly and Jill to the hospital. Take their statements there." He looked back to Tripp. "Tripp Simmons, you're under arrest for the murder of Magnolia Sweet."

He continued as Wills did the same to Tiffany. José, a deputy Molly didn't know, ushered them out of the room.

It wasn't until they were in the elevator that she made eye contact with Jill and noticed her friend had tears streaming down her face.

Molly's stomach caved in on itself and in that moment, she swore she'd never do anything to endanger anyone she loved again. Disregarding the throbbing in her body, she threw her arms around Jill.

"I'm so sorry," she said.

Jill said nothing and Molly wondered if it was too late to even hope that Jill, or Sam and his mother, would ever forgive her for getting them into this mess.

Chapter Thirty

For the second time in only a few days, Molly sat on a hospital bed in the emergency room. Apparently, showing up with the sheriff earlier in the week had sped the process along. She'd been on her own for about thirty minutes when Sam burst through the pink curtain.

"Are you okay? What the hell, Molly?" He gently cupped her face in both of his hands, bending his knees so they were eye level.

Tears sprang to her eyes. She gripped his wrists. "I'm so sorry. I have no excuses. I'm so sorry for putting Jill in danger. Have you seen her?"

He shook his head, pressing kisses to her face that she didn't feel she deserved. "No. My aunt and mom went to see her. She's down a few beds."

"Can you forgive me?" Molly whispered, tears spilling down her cheeks.

Sam tucked her against his body with extreme gentleness, mindful of her ribs, which still ached. "Do you even have to ask?"

She looked up at him. "Yes. I put her in danger and I don't know if I can forgive myself, even if Jill and you can."

"Molly," he said, smoothing her hair back from her face. "Did you force Jill to go with you?"

"No. But she wouldn't have without me," Molly said. She sniffled, trying to get control of her emotions.

"I see I have a repeat customer," Dr. Remy said, walking into the room.

Sam stepped aside and let Dr. Remy move into his place. Molly wiped her tears away.

"How you doing, Molly?" Ramona lifted her left arm and examined the scrapes and scratches from the rope.

"Been better, honestly."

"These look superficial but I'll get the nurse to clean them up. I'd like to check your ribs and we'll do another x-ray just to be sure."

"Can you prescribe bed rest?" Sam asked.

The doctor chuckled. "Would she listen?"

Molly cringed. "I might, now."

Sam laughed. "No." He met Molly's gaze. "I'm going to check on Jill. You need anything?"

"I'm fine." She tried to smile through the lie but failed. Sam assured her he'd be right back and left her alone with Dr. Remy's numerous questions and cold hands.

* * * *

She didn't see Jill until they all arrived at Katherine's, who insisted everyone come up to the bed and breakfast for some comfort food. She stopped at Calli's on the way and grabbed enough food for ten families. Tigger was overjoyed to see Molly. As if sensing she wasn't herself, he didn't jump up but stayed at her side.

Molly sat across from Jill at the long dining table, grateful when Jill reached across for her hand.

"Stop looking at me like that," Jill said.

"Like what?" Molly squeezed her hand, taking note of the rope burn along both of her friend's arms.

"Like you're wracked with guilt. It's not your fault. You didn't know. And I chose to go with you," Jill said, pulling her hand back.

Anne, Katherine, and Sam walked in carrying plates and containers of food.

"She's right," Anne said. "She's a big girl and makes her own choices. Let's just be thankful you're both okay."

"Agreed," Katherine said.

"Everyone is safe. That's all that matters," Sam said, sitting beside Molly. He kissed her cheek. "And the killer is in jail."

"I did not see that coming," Jill said. "Molly, do you think your strange reaction in the elevator was your mind's way of alerting you to trouble?"

Molly gave a half laugh. "If it was, I didn't pay very good attention."

"What happened in the elevator?" Katherine sat across from Anne.

"We ran into Tripp on the floor before Tiffany's and my head started hurting. I felt sweaty and just…off. When we were in the hotel room and I could smell his soap or cologne, it brought the attack back and I realized I'd smelled it then, too. I made the connection too late. Same with his shirt."

Three sets of eyes stared at her, but it was Anne who asked, "His shirt?"

Molly nodded, adding fries to her plate. "He had a substantial hole in his shirt and I couldn't figure out why it was bothering me. Then I remembered there was a scrap of fabric on the house on stage when we found Magnolia."

"Did he say *why*?" Katherine asked.

"He said something about money and Judd and Magnolia wrecking his plans and his life," Jill said.

Clearly, their near-death experience hadn't put a damper on any of their appetites. As they ate and chatted, Molly's guilt lessened minimally but her curiosity only increased. She just didn't understand all of the pieces and how they fit together.

"You okay?" Sam asked quietly, leaning in so his breath brushed her ear.

She squeezed his hand. "I am. I just wondered how things are going at the station."

He smiled, stroked a hand over her hair. "Of course you are."

Molly frowned. "I'm sorry."

"Don't apologize for who you are, babe. I love you. All the parts that make you *you*."

"You're too good to me," she said, leaning in for a kiss.

The chatter continued around them but Molly felt cocooned by his unconditional affection.

"Hope you still think that when I ask Chris if we can put a homing device on you so we always know your whereabouts," he joked.

Molly set her fork down. "How did he know we were there?"

The others stopped talking and looked their way. Sam pushed his plate away and folded his forearms across each other on the tabletop.

"He didn't. The warrant came through early, so they were going to search Tiffany's room. When Chris called to tell me you were on your way to the hospital, he said they'd been about to knock when they heard commotion from inside." He grinned at Molly. "He went with his gut."

"Thank goodness," Jill said. "After Molly tried to kick him in the face, I wasn't entirely sure what our next move was."

Sam groaned and dropped his head to his arms. "I did not need to know you tried to kick a killer in the face."

"Don't give her a hard time, Sam," Katherine said.

He lifted his head and sighed. Molly smiled at Katherine. "Thank you."

Katherine arched her perfectly groomed brow. "We have plenty of time to do that after you've had some rest."

The others laughed and Molly couldn't help but join in.

* * * *

Molly and Sam were getting ready for bed, Tigger trailing her every step, when their doorbell rang.

"I'll get it," Sam said over Tigger's bark.

Molly and Tigger trailed behind him. Chris stood on the other side of the door looking like the day had done a number on him.

"Hey guys, sorry to come by so late," he said.

"No problem, man. Come on in."

Sam closed the door as Chris walked over to stand in front of Molly.

"Are you okay?"

"Yes. Thank you and I'm sorry."

"You're welcome, and I know. I swear though, Molly, I don't think I've ever been as scared as when I saw the three of you huddled together, tied up and frightened." His voice held no accusation or venom. Just fact. Still, she felt comforted by Sam's presence at her side, his hand slipping into hers.

Chris looked down at their joined hands then back up at Molly. "Do you know what terrified me most?"

She shook her head, a large lump of emotion lodging in her throat.

"The idea that we might have come too late. That I would have had to tell my best friend that I didn't get there in time to save the woman he loves."

Molly pulled her hand out of Sam's and threw her arms around Chris. "I'm so sorry," she whispered.

He hugged her back, gently, and then stepped away. "I know. I'd just really like to never be in that situation again. Please."

She nodded. "Can I ask?"

He smiled, clapping Sam on the shoulder. "I'm here because I knew you would. Figured it'd be easier to come to you than have you accost me at the station tomorrow demanding an official statement."

"Come on in, man," Sam said.

They went into the living room, Molly and Sam on the couch, Chris on the armchair with Tigger in his lap.

He rubbed Tigger's head. "Hey, buddy." Tigger's ears flopped adorably, making them laugh.

"Do you want a drink or anything?" Molly asked belatedly.

Chris shook his head. "Nah. Sarah's waiting for me. You were right. Tiffany was terrified. I'm going to lay it all out there now, but I'll give you a formal statement for the paper tomorrow. You can't print all of this."

Molly's lips curled up in a grin. "Noted, Sheriff."

"Tiffany and Tripp met at the hotel where he works as a casual. He struck up a conversation with her—my guess is because he'd been stalking Magnolia and saw Tiffany at the theater—and they bonded over their mutual hatred of the woman. It complicated matters for Tiffany that she and Vivien were in love."

"I knew there was something between them," Molly said.

Chris nodded. "You were right. They kept it a secret though, because Magnolia liked to control her children's lives and frowned on workplace romances of all things. Sort of ironic considering she and Beau met on set."

"What a strange woman. But stranger is Vivien cowing to her mom's demands," Sam said. "She's a grown woman. A professional."

Tigger jumped off Chris's lap and curled up in his dog bed by the fireplace. Leaning forward, their weary friend clasped his hands between his outstretched knees.

"She is, but she was also working *for* her mother, and until she had more control over the company, she lived by Magnolia's wishes. Tiffany was scared of Magnolia but wanted to help Vivien. Magnolia could have broken Tiffany professionally and personally, so when Tripp suggested they kidnap her for ransom money, she thought it would get her out of the way for both of them."

Trying to follow the logic of that, Molly failed. "*What?*"

His tired laugh turned into a sigh. "I know. Apparently, that was the plan. Tiffany would drug Magnolia, then Tripp would kidnap her and stash her away. Without the star director, Tiffany would step up and Vivien would be able to go to the theater and see her shine. Tripp would get his money back and then some, and by the time they released Magnolia he'd be gone."

"I can't even begin to understand how they actually thought that would work," Sam said. He rubbed a hand over his face.

Molly understood his confusion. "But they didn't kidnap her."

Straightening, Chris shook his head. "Nope. Tripp never intended to. It was always about double revenge. When we called Judd down to the station and talked to him, he was shocked. Crushed and shocked. He and Tripp were supposed to start a boat launch business back in the day. They had ten grand saved. Which would have been a huge chunk and enough for them to get started. When Judd lent it to Magnolia, he swore she'd pay him back. Tripp's basically been plotting revenge ever since. While living off of Judd."

"Poor Judd," Molly said. "That's awful. So, the handkerchief of his?"

"Tripp planted it."

Sam rubbed a hand up and down Molly's arm. "What about the texts?"

"No one broke into Judd's locker. Tripp stole his phone from home. Tiffany took Magnolia's. They exchanged just enough texts to make it suspicious."

"Tripp threatened Vivien?"

Mouth pinched, Chris gave a curt nod. "Told Tiffany that if she said a word before she got him some money to leave town, he'd kill her. Since he'd killed Magnolia in cold blood, Tiffany was right not to doubt him."

"What'll happen to her?" Sam asked.

"She's an accessory to murder. And single. Judd wasn't the only one crushed. We called Jeffrey and Vivien down to the station to let them know what happened and she couldn't believe Tiffany was any part of it. They'd argued about telling her mom, but she'd never imagined Tiffany had a hand in her death. Tiffany said it wasn't meant to happen that way but I don't think Vivien will come around on the forgiveness."

As much as Tiffany had made her own bed, Molly felt a stab of empathy for the woman. Not getting the forgiveness of loved ones could really empty a person. Not that she'd know, thanks to the amazing people in her own life, but she'd worried she'd pushed things just a little too far this time.

She squeezed Sam around the middle, hanging on.

"You okay?"

She nodded. "Grateful."

He kissed her head. "You and me both."

Epilogue

The mid-May weather more than made up for the wet, cold winter, in Molly's opinion. It was hard to believe that in one month, it'd be a year since she'd come to this small town. Just a tiny point on the map fifty miles outside of Portland. When she'd shown up with everything she owned in the back of her Jeep, she'd had no way of knowing that this town, these people, would become her home.

She listened to the laughter and music of their friends who hung out on their completed deck. Sam had surprised her with overhead patio lights that made her feel like she had her very own stars.

Katherine and Brandon, who'd resumed his position as sheriff, were chatting with Sam's aunt and uncle. Chris and Sarah—who were currently looking for a place outside the heart of the city that would suit both of their needs—and an adorable Labrador pup were playing with Tigger while they chatted with Calli and Dean.

Molly had been right about the impact of Chris's job on their relationship—it took its toll but only when Chris didn't open up about it. Over lunch with Sarah, after Katherine's party, she'd found out they'd both been holding back, each afraid of pushing the other too fast.

Fear often got in the way of a lot of things, Molly realized. Gratitude filled her chest, warming her with the realization that she'd pushed past her own fears and ended up surrounded by these people.

They'd decided to have the BBQ on a Sunday evening when most of the shops and businesses were closed.

"Brought you some lemonade," Sam said, passing her a red cup with her name scratched onto it.

"Thank you. This is fun. I've never had a house party," she said. She took a sip of the yummy, ice-cold drink.

Sam stared down at her in shock. "Ever?"

Laughing, she shook her head. "No. We moved all the time. I've had friends over but I've only ever had a couple of them, even as an adult." She swept her arm out toward the yard. "Never anything like this. It's... wonderful."

Lifting his own drink, he tapped his cup against hers. "To the first of many. You can't beat a backyard BBQ. We used to do this several times throughout the summer when I was growing up. Even in my early twenties, once I got back from college, we'd all get together for big events."

"You're lucky," Molly murmured. She'd never felt like she was missing out on anything, growing up an only child and moving around a lot. She'd always been fine with her own company, something to read, and a notebook.

Now, she saw the benefit of having a tribe of people; of having an extended family and network of people who mattered. She couldn't imagine her life without any of them.

"Want some gossip?" Sam asked.

"Always."

"Jeffrey brought his Beamer in to get serviced and said that he's thinking of sticking around."

"Really?" Molly asked.

Magnolia's son had taken over directing the play, picking up where his mother and Tiffany had left off. Tiffany was currently serving jail time as an accomplice to murder, but her fear of Tripp had impacted her sentencing. Tripp wouldn't be getting out of jail in their lifetime. Vivien had left town almost immediately after the arrests were made, and they'd all been surprised when Jeffrey had remained in town after the play closed.

"Maybe he wants a fresh start," Molly murmured. He and his sister certainly deserved it.

"Speaking of," Sam said, tipping his cup in Bella's direction.

She and Gavin were playing bocce on the lawn with Alan, his wife, Elizabeth, and John Granger. When John had shown up, they'd all hoped Corky would too, but John said he was content just hanging out in the barn with the cats.

Bella tipped her head back and laughed at something Gavin said. He was working out great at the paper and had formally accepted a full-time staff position earlier this month. They both claimed to be just friends, and though they probably were, there was no denying the spark between them.

"She deserves it, too." Molly leaned into Sam.

"Agreed. Speaking of things we deserve," he said, sliding his arm around her.

Tipping her head back she met his gaze and waited.

"Tigger mentioned this morning that he thinks he deserves a companion." Sam's lips pursed with humor.

"Is that so?" Molly chuckled.

"Yeah. He had all these reasons and I just couldn't think of one argument against it. Told him I'd talk to you."

"Did he have anything in mind?"

Sam's smile grew. "Actually, I don't know how he heard, but friends of the Grangers have almost ready-to-go Maltese puppies."

Molly shook her head and pretended to think about things. "He must have his paw on the animal grapevine."

Laughter lit up Sam's eyes. "Guess so." He took a deep breath. Let it out. "We could go look at them."

"How soon?" Molly asked, grinning so wide her cheeks ached.

Sam's subtle blush made her heart flutter. He met her gaze. "I told them we'd swing by tomorrow?"

Happiness washed over her and her loud laughter brought Tigger running. As Molly wrapped her arms around Sam's neck, hugging him close, Tigger wedged between them and flopped on their feet. Looked like their family would be growing.

Printed in the United States
by Baker & Taylor Publisher Services